Hoofbeats

Lara at Athenry Castle

Book Three

by KATHLEEN DUEY

PUFFIN BOOKS

PUFFIN BOOKS
Published by the Penguin Group
Penguin Young Readers Group, 345 Hudson Street,
New York, New York 10014, U.S.A.
Penguin Group (Canada), 10 Alcorn Avenue, Toronto, Ontario,
Canada M4V 3B2 (a division of Pearson Penguin Canada Inc.)
Penguin Books Ltd, 80 Strand, London WC2R 0RL, England
Penguin Ireland, 25 St Stephen's Green, Dublin 2, Ireland
(a division of Penguin Books Ltd)
Penguin Group (Australia), 250 Camberwell Road, Camberwell,
Victoria 3124, Australia (a division of Pearson Australia Group Pty Ltd)
Penguin Books India Pvt Ltd, 11 Community Centre,
Panchsheel Park, New Delhi - 110 017, India
Penguin Group (NZ), Cnr Airborne and Rosedale Roads, Albany,
Auckland 1310, New Zealand (a division of Pearson New Zealand Ltd)
Penguin Books (South Africa) (Pty) Ltd, 24 Sturdee Avenue,
Rosebank, Johannesburg 2196, South Africa

Penguin Books Ltd, Registered Offices: 80 Strand,
London WC2R 0RL, England

Published simultaneously in the United States of America by Dutton Children's
Books and Puffin Books, divisions of Penguin Young Readers Group, 2005

1 3 5 7 9 10 8 6 4 2

Copyright © Kathleen Duey, 2005
All rights reserved.

Puffin Books ISBN 0-14-240220-6

Printed in the United States of America

For Star, a dapple-gray Welsh pony, with a true five-point white star on his side. He was the smartest pony I have ever known. I met him in a dark pasture, in a driving rain, on the night he was born. Birth is a fierce, joyous miracle. Anyone who falls in love with a newborn foal is permanently touched, forever changed, forever grateful.

CHAPTER ONE

❧ ❧ ❧

*I do not want to leave my mother. Why won't these men let
me turn back? I will keep calling to her.
She will find me.
I know she will.*

I stood alone in the middle of the meadow.
My heart was breaking.

The sound of Dannsair's terrified whinnying
was fading. I could see the last of the baron's long
line of riders disappearing uphill into the mist.
One of them held my filly's halter strap, dragging
her along, taking her away from me.

In the opposite direction, there were three
riders cantering downhill through the fog on
their way back to the barns. Conall had said I
could come back, at least until my aunt Fallon

decided whether or not she would marry Brian. If she did, there would be trouble; he was an enemy of my father's.

Or I could simply go home to my own tuath. My mother would be so glad to see me, to know I had not been harmed, and I missed Bebinn and Gerroc. All our lives we had been as close as sisters, as peas in a pod.

My bare feet pink with cold, I stood there, trying not to cry. There was no time for it. I had to decide what I was going to do—and quickly.

I *wanted* to return to the great circle of ancient earthen walls at home. I loved my family, after all. And as mean as my father often was, I knew he loved me. Where was he now? Looking for Fallon and me? Not likely. He was probably off fighting somewhere—there were always more battles in summertime.

I wiped mist and tears from my face and stared downhill at the three riders. If I went back with them to Conall's barns, I would not be allowed to work with the horses. He and Cormac's father had let me care for Dannsair because she had taken me as a foster mother when her dam died.

No other foal would be trusted to me. I would not be allowed to ride. Conall fostered *boys* to teach them the skills of horse care, not girls. None of them except Cormac had tried to be my friend. Even though it had all gone wrong, he had at least tried to help me escape.

Dannsair's whinnying was very slowly growing softer with distance. They were not riding fast. Why would they? They had no reason to hurry, and for that I was grateful. I listened, imagining my poor filly's fear. My fists balled up, and my eyes stung again. She would be trained and ridden by men and boys, not by me. And she would be ridden to war unless I could save her.

It seemed to me that the faeries and the saints had given Dannsair to me, even if my father and two other men thought she belonged to them.

And there it was. My heart had spoken.

Dannsair was my own.

Think what they might, the men were all wrong.

Dannsair had depended on me to bring her into this world. She had looked to me to keep her safe and to see that she was fed and warm. She had trusted me the way a child trusts her mother.

I could barely stand the fading sound of her frightened whinnying. Still, I waited a little longer before I tightened the thick cloak Cormac had given me. I reached inside the neck of my leine to touch the little gold horse pin I had found between the high walls of our rath, hoping it would bring me luck. Then I took a deep breath to steady my quaking heart.

When the last of the baron's riders had been swallowed up by the mist and Dannsair's cries were faded nearly to silence, I started walking.

Maybe one day I would go home. I hoped so. I longed to see my family.

Perhaps I would someday see Conall and Cormac and the wonderful long barns full of beautiful horses again.

But for now, I had to follow Dannsair.

She needed me.

CHAPTER TWO

✵ ✵ ✵

The darkness is full of sounds and scents I do not know.
The other horses do not seem afraid, but I cannot
sleep for listening. Where is my mother?

The mist was so thick that it wet my hair. I tore a thin strip of the yellow brat to tie it back and left it bound. I had no comb.

I had planned my escape with Dannsair. I had imagined stopping at farms, begging help or doing work to earn a little bread. I had *not* imagined that the Baron of Athenry would meet us on the path and take my filly.

As it was, of course, I couldn't stop when I heard voices or spied donkeys burdened with bundles of cut barley with boys my age walking behind, driving the animals along. I could not ask where they lived or if their tuath would welcome a wayfarer. I would not be able to take even an hour to seek a meal to quiet my rumbling stomach. I was afraid to lose Dannsair.

I knew the baron and his men were going to Athenry Castle, but I had no idea where it was, except that it sat beside a ford on the Clareen River. I had no idea where the Clareen River was; I only knew that my father had once said it was deep and wide.

I worried and hurried at first, but it wasn't too hard to keep up; they rode at an easy pace. When I fell behind, I could follow their horses' tracks until I heard voices again.

Walking along in the wet and chill, my bare feet half numb, I tried to recall every single thing my father had ever said about Athenry. He traveled there once each year to pay our tuath's share of our cheese, meat, and my mother's fine blue cloth to the baron. He had once had a sword made there. He is not a long-winded storyteller, my father, but I had lain awake one night and listened as my mother asked him questions to keep him talking more.

As I followed the baron and his men—and my Dannsair—I tried to recall everything he had said.

It wasn't much:

The Normans ruled it. There was a stone castle where the Baron of Athenry and his family lived, my father had said. Its walls were high and thick, and it jutted out from the town wall like a rounded point of land juts out into the sea.

The town wall enclosed a great wide meadow. There was a market square and many smaller buildings of wattle and daub—enough for our whole tuath several times over.

There was a Dominican priory with arches and peaked windows where the priests lived—my father often made food gifts to them as well.

There was a stone church being built and a great stone cross in the market square that was tall as a ten-years boy.

There was an Irish swordmaker who had traded my father a grand sword for a cow and an ell of my mother's blue cloth.

And last, the Baron of Athenry was cruel to beggars.

That was all.

I dredged my memory and could find no more.

That night I slept beneath a thick-trunked oak. I woke stiff and chilly and ate my bit of cheese and bread, listening until I heard faint voices from the baron's camp. When they began to travel, I followed.

Dannsair still whinnied, but not nearly so much. It was clear she was losing hope that I would come to her. I cannot describe the pain that caused me. I longed to comfort her and lead her away from the men. But I knew it was impossible.

By midmorning of the third day, I had settled into a pattern. I was careful to keep to the edge of the woods where I could, and to drop back when the path passed over open meadows.

I gathered fistfuls of lamb's-quarters, cress, and herbs as I walked, to have something to eat with my bits of cheese and hard bread. Now and then I found a few late hazelnuts that I could crack at night between stones.

One afternoon, I found a patch of lamb's-quarters and a fleshy clump of mushrooms and spent the rest of the day wishing I were home, helping my mother around the evening fire. I ached for a bed of dry straw and a warm meal of buttered mushrooms and steaming venison or roast pork. This year, I would be far from home for the Feast of Samhain.

One evening, the baron and his men didn't stop for the night until it was nearly dark. Tired, I laid out my cloak, then lay upon it and fell fast asleep, exhausted from walking and worrying. The ground was hard and uncomfortable, and I was restless, turning over and over most the night, I think. I must have.

Near morning, I woke to a painful scratching on my scalp. In the failing light, I had chosen a burr patch to sleep in. I tried to pull the hook-spined burrs out of my hair, but only made things worse. Half asleep and furious, I sat up and tried to undo the strip of yellow linen I had used to tie back my hair and couldn't work it free. My tail of hair was a mass of burrs.

I was startled out of my silent fury when I heard voices from the baron's camp. I rose quickly, wincing when I turned my head and the burrs prickled at my scalp.

I spent the morning picking burrs off my woolen cloak as I walked. I spent the afternoon working at my hair. I managed to get a few burrs out—not many.

Trying to sleep was a misery that night. By the next evening, the burrs had become torturous, digging at my scalp. Desperate, I found a smooth stone and ground an edge on the shard of bronze I had found in Conall's barn so long before. By midmorning, it was sharp-edged as a knife.

That evening, once the baron and his men had made camp and I could stop, I cut out the burrs. I had to cut most of my hair very close. I scraped my scalp bloody more than once. In the few places where there were no burrs, I cut my hair anyway, just to even it out.

All the while, I kept thinking about how careful my mother had been, all my life, to make sure that I combed my hair, that I took some care to keep it neat. I missed her so much that when I cried, I wasn't sure whether it was the pain of the burrs and the knife—or my homesickness.

That night it began to rain, and it turned cold. Cormac's cloak kept me alive on that long journey, plain and true. Without it, I would have shivered myself into illness, sleeping in the open. I wanted to thank him one day.

Thinking that, I felt odd for a moment, and it puzzled me. Then I realized what the feeling was, and I blushed. I had been angry at Cormac. Even though he hadn't meant to betray me, his advice had guided me straight into the Baron of Athenry's path. I hoped to see Cormac again—and it had little to do with thanking him. I liked him.

I remembered Bebinn and Tally, smiling at each other, then blushed again, embarrassed by my own foolishness. If I was going to be drawn to a boy, surely I had more sense about it than my aunt Fallon—Cormac was the younger brother of Fallon's beloved Brian. They were both sons of a man my father hated, an enemy.

I ate only small bits of my food to stretch it. My hunger would not keep me from following Dannsair any more than our usual winter hunger had stopped me from working at home. I was used to having an empty belly—though not usually this time of year. At home, there would still be plenty of cheese and milk, and last month's harvest of wheat and barley meant bread in every house. Thoughts of food made my mouth water. I stopped thinking about it.

I often got close enough to see Dannsair. The rope was slack now. She was smart and had learned that dragging at it was useless. She carried her head high and proud, and her gait was like her mother's had been, graceful and swift. Now and then she would stop and turn to look back down the path as if she knew I was following.

I knew if I called her name she would try to run toward me. But the men would chase her down. She was only a weanling after all; we could not outrun their horses.

As I had so many times at Conall's barns, I longed for her to grow up, to be able to carry me, swift as wind, so that no one could keep us anywhere against our will, ever again.

The tracks joined a path, then the path became wider and deeper. It diverged into two tracks that ran parallel over the land. I saw four carts in the distance that day.

The paths near my home were thin, not wide enough for two people, much less two horses.

Later that day, I smelled bitter forge smoke. We had to be getting closer to Athenry.

My first glimpse of the castle came from between the branches of a holly tree. I had climbed it to see what direction the baron and his men were taking, to see if I should run and catch up or if I should stay back.

Framed by stiff, prickly holly leaves, I saw a wide meadow full of late-summer grass. The little caravan of horses and men leading Dannsair away from me were crossing it, headed toward an arched gate set into the stone walls of Athenry town. The Clareen River ran through it on the east side.

The castle amazed me. As my father had said, it jutted out from the town wall. From my tree, it looked like a small circle perched on the edge of a much larger one. Its walls were a good deal higher than the town walls, and much thicker. It was the biggest building I had ever seen, by far. It seemed impossible that stone could be laid that high without it falling in. There was a strange slanting wall all around its base, like a vast apron of smooth stone.

The gate was wide enough for the riders to remain side by side. I could see the arches and peaked windows of the priory by the river and a cluster of houses and byres sprawling across the enclosed fields behind it.

The baron and his men cantered across the cleared land, and I could only watch, my eyes filling with tears, as they neared the gate. This was the end of my journey.

They were taking Dannsair where I could not follow. She reared as the monstrous wooden doors creaked open. The men laughed at her. She whinnied, wrenching around against the pull of the rope to look back toward the edge of the woods where I stood, hidden in the shadows.

I believe this: She knew I was there. She had known all along. She could scent me or sense me— or perhaps she just knew me well enough to know that I would never leave her alone with strangers.

When I did not call back to her from the woods, she turned and went quietly through the gates. When they closed, I thought my heart would stop. I had to find a way inside.

CHAPTER THREE

✤ ✤ ✤

I am in a dark place with many other horses again. There
is enough food for all of us, it seems, but I am lonely,
and I am frightened. Why has my mother not come?

efore the sun went down to begin the new
day, I found a trickling stream for water
and washing, and I had made a mound of loose
grass for my bed. Upstream, I found a thick patch
of cress and ate my very last bit of saved cheese.
Then I fell onto my grass pallet, and for once I was
asleep before I had time to worry about anything.

The next morning, I went back to the holly
tree and climbed higher than I had before so I
could better watch Athenry Castle and the town
that had grown up around it.

There were several gates in the wall; I could see three and was sure there were probably one or two more along the far end. I saw the guards let in merchants' carts and four huntsmen returning with deer slung over a packhorse's saddle.

I was amazed as I watched the town waking up. People were walking paths between the houses, clearing ground for gardens, gathering in what had to be the market square. More people lived in and around Athenry than I had ever imagined. It could not possibly be a single tuath.

The castle wasn't the only huge stone building, just as my father had said. I could see the priory where monks and priests lived more clearly now. There were stoneworkers beginning the walls of what I thought was the church.

I knew that the Baron of Athenry was a Norman, come here from England with the king's permission to rule over us. I could see many Normans inside the walls. But a lot of the people of Athenry looked to be Irishmen. I saw them coming and going from the whitewashed houses that stood inside the stone walls.

The Normans, of course, I could tell by their leggings and bright tunics, even at a distance. I had seen them when they had come adventuring through the wilds of Connaught, then on to the sea's edge in Connemara.

I envied them, just then, hungry as I was. *Their* adventures never seemed to include putting up with an empty belly. More than once, they had claimed their right—as relatives of the Norman Baron of Athenry—to ask our hospitality.

They had often eaten far too much of our precious stored food before they traveled on. The Normans did not return the favor of hospitality to poor travelers, I soon saw. Every morning a few beggars had been thrown from the gates, then were driven off with sticks and threats.

It scared me, true.

I looked no different from most of them, ragged and soiled. Most were grown and a few were old—but some were as young as I was.

I sat in my holly tree, my back against the smooth trunk, my leine pulled close, my brat tight around my shoulders to protect me from the prickly leaves. It was not comfortable, but it was a fine tree, tall as the sky, almost. From its height, I could see Irishmen working.

There were metalsmiths and stonecutters and bone carvers with piles of antlers and skulls outside their houses. I saw bundles of wool brought in carts; there were spinners and weavers in Athenry.

The next day I watched the baron's hunting party go past. And later that day, I watched the people celebrate. It was the first Samhain of my life spent alone, and I hoped it would be the last. I wept with homesickness as much as hunger when I smelled the cooking in the air.

The Samhain Feast in the town seemed muted and quiet to me. There were bonfires, but they were small. I heard little shouting or laughter. I saw a priest walk up from the priory before it got dark, his long black robes swirling in the little breeze. He performed a prayer, then the people went back to their houses. And so summer passed into winter as quietly as I had ever seen it. Gam had begun and it would soon turn cold.

In all my life, I had never seen Norman girls or women. One sunny morning a group of them came out of the arched gate, walking arm in arm. They looked, from a distance, like a bouquet of flowers scattered on the stiff autumn grass. They wore dresses of colors and shapes I could never have dreamed of, of silk so thin it floated on the air like a cupped leaf floats on water. Long sleeves trailed from their elbows nearly to the ground. They wore hats of rolled silk and shawls of fine wool.

I stared as they laughed and talked—and walked within a stone's throw of where I was hiding.

One was talking about learning to make blood pudding. Another complained about a mean cousin. They sounded like anyone, like every girl I had ever known. Then I heard the one with the lightest hair say she wanted to go riding soon. That confounded me. Did Norman girls ride for pleasure? Were they *allowed*?

Too soon, they were past me, three of them hooking arms and tilting their heads close to whisper. Their easy laughter made a sadness bloom inside my heart. I missed my mother. I missed Bebinn and Gerroc and Magnus and everyone else in my tuath. My eyes filled with tears.

I longed to tell Bebinn and Gerroc about Dannsair. I wanted to tell them about Fallon and how her love of Brian had made her so much nicer. I wanted to whisper to Bebinn that I liked Cormac—even though it was impossible since our fathers were enemies. It would be hard enough for Fallon. My father would never let his own sister marry an enemy—and it would be a year *after* never that he would allow his daughter to do the same.

I wept a long time, from loneliness. What had I done, coming so far from home, so far from my family? Then I wondered what the gowned Norman girls would think if they could see me in my dirty, outgrown leine with my ugly, chopped-off hair, and I cried a little more.

That night I lay awake on my mat of grass, listening to the creek, staring up through the branches at the stars. My belly was churning with hunger, and I was no closer to Dannsair than if I had never followed her.

The next day, I watched two carts go through the gates. They were loaded with what looked like client payment. I saw wrapped rounds of cheese, sacks of grain, and chickens in a wooden cage.

For the first time in my life, I wondered how many tuatha paid food and goods in tribute to the Baron of Athenry. How big were the storage chambers in the castle? Did the Normans ever go hungry? Did people in their families die in the winter for lack of food?

The next day, I washed my soiled leine. There were snags and tiny holes in the fabric. It had been worn when I arrived at the barns where Conall and the rí were breeding their warhorses. It was much worse now. The bushes and thickets had taken their toll.

I wrung it out and wore it wet until it dried. Longing for a little color in my old clothing, I tore three long, thin strips from my old yellow brat and braided them into a belt. The brat was half its former size. I had used it to dry foals, and had torn strips from it and an old leine to make Dannsair's first halter. What was left of it was soft with use, but still strong. The braided belt was rough, but it covered two of the worst tears.

Being clean lifted my spirits.

But it did not solve my problem.

I was so hungry that I knew I would soon

become weak. It was only a matter of time before one of the baron's hounds noticed my stranger's scent and led the hunters to me. I would have no chance of escape.

I had to think of some way to enter the gates of Athenry. Maybe when the girls were out walking again, I could approach them and explain about Dannsair. But would any of them help me? More likely, they would tell their fathers, and I would be caught.

My thoughts were scattered by voices coming from deep in the woods. I ran to gather up my cloak and scatter the grass bed I had made. I barely had time to climb into the lowest branches of my holly tree before two boys came into the clearing. I held very still, my heart pounding.

CHAPTER FOUR

❧ ❧ ❧

*I wait, always, for the sound of my mother's soft voice,
her gentle hands. There is food here, in plenty, and I have
the comfort of many horses close to me. But am I
to be here forever? Will I never see my mother again?*

They were Normans, wearing leggings and deep red coats that covered them to their knees. The older one looked angry and mean. The younger one was trying not to cry. He was clearly angry, too, breathing so hard he could barely stand straight. Even so, he managed to herd seven pigs along in front of him, tapping them with a rod of peeled oak.

"You ran when you saw the wolf," the older boy accused him.

"I did not," the younger boy defended himself. "I was trying to get the pigs away."

"Niall!" the older boy shouted. "Another wolf!"

The younger boy spun around to look—and the older one burst into derisive laughter. Then he frowned. "If you tell Father I napped, I will tell him you are scared of shadows in the trees."

The younger boy glared at him. "You never do your share."

The older boy shrugged. "Do you want him to know you are a coward, Niall?"

"I am not a coward," Niall said quietly.

I understood how he felt. My aunt Fallon had been mean to me all my life. She is only five years older than I am, having been born when my grandmother was getting old.

Niall looked up at the older boy. "I will tell Father you sleep while I work."

The older boy's face darkened. Abruptly, he ran forward, shouting and waving his arms. Startled, the pigs scattered and ran, squealing, disappearing into the trees.

Grinning, the older boy faced Niall. "Explain that to Father. I will tell him I was chasing off wolves, and you lost the pigs because you ran, crying like a baby."

With that, he went off. Niall stood still, and I could tell by his hunched shoulders that he was about to cry. I meant to stay hidden until he left, but my right foot slipped on the branch, and I had to grab a handful of twigs to steady myself.

Niall turned and looked up. His eyes widened, and he stared at me. "Who are you?"

I had no idea what to say.

"Who are you?" he repeated. "I have never seen you before."

"I will help you find the pigs," I told him.

He tipped his head to stare at me. "You don't live in Athenry, do you?"

"I have come from the west," I said. Then I took a deep breath. "I am near to starving, hoping to find work in Athenry. I am not a beggar," I added. Then I shut my mouth. I did not want to tell him my story. It was too long and too strange. He wouldn't believe me—or if he did, he would tell someone.

"Help me find all twelve pigs, and I will make sure you eat this night in Athenry," Niall said.

I blinked, surprised. "I offered help without expecting reward," I told him. "But I thank you. Can you do that, truly?"

He nodded and stood straighter. "I know all the guards." He met my eyes. "Where you come from, do boys swear oaths and then clasp hands?"

I nodded. I had seen my brothers do it.

"Will you give me your word, then? You won't steal a pig? You will help me honorably?"

I nodded again. "You have my word."

He stepped forward, extending his hand. He grasped mine and lifted it, staring straight into my eyes. "And you have mine. Help me, and I will make sure you have supper tonight in my father's house."

I could not help but lower my hand awkwardly, and I hoped he wouldn't notice. Because of my close-cut hair and my outgrown knee-length leine, he thought I was a boy. And because he thought that, he had asked me for my word and bond. I was not about to set him straight and lose a chance to get past the gates of Athenry.

It did not take us long to find the pigs. The woods were thick with fallen logs, and they hadn't run too far before common sense had stopped them. I found seven pigs, one a squealing young sow in a hazelnut bush that was hard to drive until she realized that all the pigs were going in the same direction.

Niall had found six. He smiled and thanked me warmly. He now had one more pig than he had started out with that morning. That would please his father, he said.

It was easy to tell which was the wild pig as we started across the meadow toward the gates. It was the young sow I had found. She thought better of letting us drive her forward about halfway across the meadow.

With Niall and me running back and forth to cut off her paths of escape and the rest of the pigs trotting forward willingly, we made it to the gate to find the guards laughing at our efforts.

Niall nodded at them as we went past. I saw one of them look at me twice, but he said nothing.

My heart leaped. Dannsair was in here somewhere. Now I would be able to find her. I exhaled long and slow, then I noticed Niall studying me. "Will you tell me your story one day?"

I could only stare at him.

He tapped the hindmost pig gently with his stick and then glanced at me. "How you got here, I mean."

"It's a dull tale," I said, hoping to end it there, but he shook his head.

"I doubt that." He sighed. "I will never see anyplace but Athenry if my father has his way. And he will, of course."

I lowered my head and concentrated on keeping the wild sow with the others.

"He wants me to be an account keeper for the Baron of Athenry. That's how he earns our bread. He counts wheat sheaves, chickens, ells of cloth, baskets of hazelnuts, and whatever else the people pay the baron."

I nodded to let him know I was listening, but I tell you true: Athenry was so full of noise, scents, and sights that I wasn't, not really. There were so many voices, so many people going in so many directions—and all I wanted to see was my moon-colored filly.

"My father counts things. All day long," Niall said quietly, and there was so much dread in his voice that I understood at last. Contrary to his brother's taunts, the thing Niall feared most was boredom.

The lane took us past the back side of the castle, close enough to see the smooth, slanted base of the stone walls. Their purpose was obvious. No man could set a ladder or climb the walls to attack.

The castle was *huge*—taller than the holly tree, much bigger than it had looked from a distance. I felt like a wood louse looking up at an oak tree.

Niall and the pigs set a pace too fast for me to gawp at everything we passed—the tall stone arches of the priory, the rising church—it was all astounding to me.

I hurried to keep up, my tight, aching stomach reminding me that Niall had promised food. Oh, how I hoped he had meant it, but even if he hadn't, I was overjoyed at being inside the gates at last. We kept walking, passing into a maze of paths that ran between houses much like the ones at home, but bigger and more grand.

"At least tell me your name," Niall said.

When he spoke, I was looking at a weaver's

byre, long hanks of spun wool and flax hanging from the walls. I turned to face him, feeling foolish. Of course he would ask my name. So would others. And I had given my answer no thought at all.

He met my eyes. "For my father. He will want to know."

I nodded, thinking desperately. I could not tell him my real name, of course. I had to use a boy's name. After a long and awkward silence, I borrowed my youngest brother's.

"Trian," I said, trying to sound as though I had only paused out of caution, not confusion.

Niall nodded, then pointed. "There. That is my father's house."

I followed his gesture and caught my breath. It was a grand place. The house itself was three or four times as big as my father's house, and there was a byre for the pigs and another, longer one that probably held cows or a horse or two. There was a garden in front of the place, and I saw two young girls pulling weeds. It made me homesick, and I stared at the girls until Niall spoke.

"Is something wrong?"

I shook my head and squared my shoulders as a boy might have done. "Do we put the pigs in the byre?"

"No." He pointed. I followed his gesture and saw a pen behind the byre. It was like no paling I had ever seen. Instead of driving slender branches into the earth close together so that the pigs could not get out, they had used the stout branches and driven them in an arm's length apart. Then they had woven dried rushes into them; it made a sort of basketry wall. There was a gate that swung on leather hinges.

The wild sow was panicked at first, and I was afraid she might slam into the woven paling and break through, but she didn't. She began nosing in the dirt for something worth eating.

"She might have been raised in a byre, then went wild," I said.

"Perhaps," a man said from behind us.

I started and turned to see a tall Norman man wearing a fine, long Irish wool cloak over his tunic and leggings. It looked odd to see Irish and Norman clothing mixed like that. I realized I was staring at him and looked aside.

"Where did you find him, Niall?" the man said.

"Fintan scattered the pigs in the woods, and Trian offered to help me."

The man nodded, and I felt his eyes on me. I squared my shoulders again and stood with my feet apart like my brothers did.

"Where are you from, Trian?" he asked me. "Where is your family?"

I heard Niall clear his throat. He was looking at his father, making a tiny gesture, frowning, his eyes sad. "He hasn't eaten proper in days," Niall said.

His father made a small sound of sympathy. "Another Irish orphan," he said.

I held my tongue. It was clear that he did not think much of the Irish. Did he know how many Irish hated the Normans?

"Too many tuatha can't even feed their own children," he added. There was disgust in his voice.

Now, *that* made me angry.

We did half starve sometimes, but it wasn't because we didn't work hard and store every bit of food that we could. I had heard my father say the reason we had so little food during Gam's cold months was that the Normans demanded too much in tribute payments.

"Father?" Niall said, breaking the silence. "I owe Trian a debt of honor—and he is very hungry."

Niall's father smiled. "Take him in to your mother. Tomorrow, he will need to find other work. I have no use for another boy."

I resented being talking about as though I were a dog that didn't understand what they were saying. But I thanked Niall's father, then followed Niall into the house. His mother gave me a bowl of oatmeal and half a hard-cooked egg, then went on about her work and did not watch me, so I ate like a wolf, in quick, huge bites. When she saw that I had licked the bowl clean, she filled it a second time.

I cleaned a chicken byre that afternoon, and she fed me again at dark. That night I slept beside the chicken byre on a mound of clean stable bedding, warm beneath the cloak that Cormac had given me. I slept so heavily that not even the roosters could wake me before the sun was fully up.

CHAPTER FIVE

❧ ❧ ❧

It is so hard to stand all day in this place where there is no room to run, no room to play. I can hear rain. I can smell it. If my mother were here, we would go walking in it together.

I bid Niall and his mother farewell in the morning. They were kind, but Niall made me uneasy. He was too curious, too eager to hear about my travels—and his father worked for the Baron of Athenry.

Even as I said my good-byes and thanked them for their kindness, I kept catching Niall looking at me—*studying* me. I worried that he suspected I wasn't a boy—or at least that I was not simply a beggar-orphan forced by hunger to go adventuring. I think he wanted me to be something exciting, like a tale told late at night.

I didn't want him studying my face and asking questions, searching for clues. If he figured out I was a girl, he would probably tell someone. And that person would whisper it to someone else. In my own tuath, whispers traveled faster than the swiftest horse.

Or, even worse, if I managed to do what I had come to Athenry to try to do—and I escaped with my filly—he might take small things I said and be able to patch them together to know where my tuath was. The Baron of Athenry could cause terrible trouble for my family if he were angry with me.

Niall *wanted* a life of adventure. I did not. I just wanted to be near Dannsair again, to take care of her and find someplace we could both call home.

For two days after I left Niall's house, I walked the crooked paths between the buildings of Athenry, trying to see Dannsair. I was careful not to bother anyone, not to seem as though I was begging.

It was hard.

My leine was outgrown and tattered, and the

belt I had braided was ragged. My cloak, because it was dark brown, looked much better—I pulled it closed across my chest. I saw some of the Norman women glance my way, frowning. But I saw them frown at many of the Irish children, especially those of us poorly dressed.

I saw Niall now and then, too, but managed either to wave and be off in a different direction, or to keep him from seeing me at all. I wondered what had happened between him and his brother. I wondered who their father had believed. I wished him well. If things had been different, I would liked to have been his friend. As things were, I could not.

As strange as it sounds, I was not able to find the baron's stables as I wandered through the paths and pastures of Athenry town. I began to fear that the horses were not kept in the stone-walled town, but were behind the high walls of the castle itself.

If they were, I had no idea what I would do. I had watched the castle gates. There were guards posted all the time, and the gates were opened only to let soldiers, guards, or guests of the baron pass.

I finally risked asking an old, poorly dressed

man where the baron kept his horses. He smiled and pointed at the far end of the town walls. I followed his gesture and felt a weight of despair settle on my shoulders. It was better than inside the castle, but only barely.

There was a high paling that enclosed a big section of the open land on the south side of the town. I had noticed it and thought it was their grain fields, fenced high to keep out cattle and pigs.

The paling was the kind I was used to, with smooth branches the width of a woman's arm set in a line in the ground, driven into the hard earth so close together that no one could see inside and only mice could find a way to pass.

There was a gate in the fence—but only one. The Baron of Athenry was careful of his horses, it seemed. Walking beyond the buildings and the maze of paths that ran between them, I got close enough to see that a guard stood beside it.

It took me three or four days to gather my courage, but I walked the length of the town and approached the guard very politely. I asked him if I could clean stalls for a bit of bread each day.

He shrugged. "It is the stablemaster you must ask, not me."

"How would I find him, sir?" I asked, keeping my eyes down and my voice even and courteous.

"He has little use for beggars," the guard said, "but you can ask if you dare. He comes here every morning just after sunrise. He is tall, and his hair is the color of wheat straw."

I thanked him and walked away, my heart aching. I had come so far and I wanted to see Dannsair so badly, and I had dared to hope that today might be the day. I could not hold back my tears.

Three Norman boys wearing clean, bright tunics noticed me weeping. They laughed, then called out insults. I ignored them until they began to throw stones, then I ran from them. I could hear them laughing for a long ways.

It was an odd thing. They called me a weepy girl, shouting *girl* as an insult. Even though they were taunting me about crying the way they would taunt any boy they decided to pick on—it made me feel strange. I was a girl, after all, and crying just seemed *right* sometimes.

That evening, I went to the weaver's house I had noticed my first day in Athenry. The weaver let me sweep the flax and wool lint from his floors and gave me a bowl of porridge. Then he bid me gone.

I slept that night behind a pile of antlers and cow bones behind a carver's house. I went there in the dark and left before the dawn. He had no dogs—I had made sure of that—but he was a fierce-looking man, and I had not asked permission.

The next day I helped an old woman shell dried peas. She gave me bread and boiled cabbage. Her garden was big, and her family was small. She told me I could sleep in her little garden byre with her goats if I pulled weeds each day.

I was glad to make the bargain. The goats were tame and gentle. Besides trying to chew on the cloak Cormac had given me, they were very pleasant company.

Every morning I went to watch the stable-yard gate. On the fourth day, I saw the stablemaster. I ran forward, starting to speak, but he lifted one hand in a gesture of dismissal so final that I might as well have been a fly he wanted to shoo away.

The guard shook his head when I glanced at him after the gate had closed in my face. Then he looked away. I walked off, trying not to cry again. I didn't know what to do next.

Should I keep trying to talk to the stable-master? What if he got angry and forced me to leave like the beggars I had seen pushed out of the main gates?

I was *not* a beggar. I was able and willing to work. I would have cleaned every byre in the town for the chance to see Dannsair. But no one would give me that chance.

The next morning, I went about finding work so I could eat, pulling weeds that evening to pay for a place to sleep in the goat shed that night. By the third night, I knew the weeds would be gone in seven or eight days, and I would need to look elsewhere for my shelter.

I avoided the three Norman boys and Niall as I looked for work and a place to live. The cold rains of Gam were not too far off. But as often as I could, I watched the stable gate. Twice I saw it open, and a man on horseback leading three young horses came through. It made sense. The weanlings needed exercise.

Both times, the man rode across the meadow just inside the town wall to stay away from the houses and noise of Athenry town. He headed straight toward the North Gate—the one I had come through with Niall.

Once he was outside the town walls, he swung a wide right turn and doubled back, following the natural fall of the land, finally veering off to go uphill, where he disappeared over a ridge.

Seeing the horses being exercised gave me hope. If I watched long enough, surely I would be looking at the right moment to see Dannsair. After that day, I began to spend every waking moment I could watching the gate.

One fine morning, after seven days of watching, I chanced to be looking at the right moment. As always, I held my breath when the gate opened.

And when I saw Dannsair, her lovely head held high, I felt my heart leap. She had grown! Her flanks were full, and her coat was clean. A burden eased from my heart.

As the rider cantered toward the North Gate,

I held my breath and bit my lip. Dannsair was playing, tossing her head. She surged ahead, and the rider had to urge his horse and the other two half-grown colts to keep up.

It was all I could do not to call out Dannsair's name. I wanted to touch her silken coat and feel her grass-scented breath along my cheek. I wanted to call her and have her gallop to me.

But of course I could not.

I could only stand there and watch from a distance as the rider led her and the other two weanlings out the gates and back around to head up the long rise toward the ridge—and out of sight.

I exhaled, feeling everything all at once. I was relieved and furious and sad and joyous. I stood flat-footed, my shoulders squared as I was learning to do in order to look like a boy. But as I stood staring after my filly, I could not help but cry.

I heard catcalls and knew without turning that the three Norman boys had noticed me again. They could not see my tears this time. They were calling me lazy, asking why I wasn't somewhere working for my bread and a new leine.

Careful not to move my shoulders much, I

kept my back to them and used the tail of my braided sash to wipe my eyes dry.

I had no idea why boys did not cry so much as girls, but I was learning that they taunted any boy who did. I *had* to learn not to weep every time my feelings rose like a sea tide inside me or someone would discover my secret.

I squared my shoulders. Boys learned how not to cry, so I could, too. I had to. I dragged in a long slow breath, set my face like stone, and walked off. The boys shouted at me, so I glared at them over my shoulder. They did not chase me.

It rained more often as Gam settled its chill over the land. The paths were often muddy. Many of the people in the town had leathern shoes and leggings to keep the cold and wet from their skin. I envied them. Many days passed between the times I was able to see Dannsair. It pulled at my heart, but I could not spend all of every single day watching for her—or I would starve.

At first, it hadn't been too hard to find someone willing to trade a meal for a day's work. Now it was harder. The nights were cold, and people began to hoard food against a long winter.

It would only get more difficult to find work, I knew. It might become impossible.

I longed to find a way into the stables. I wished I could sleep next to Dannsair as I had in Conall's barns. I could simply climb the fence, but if I was caught doing that, I might have to face a justiciar for punishment—which might bring my father into the problem if he was called to the baron's courts.

The punishments were severe—any trespass or theft fine would be very high—it was the baron I was up against after all.

At the very least, I would be forced to leave Athenry forever, and I would not be able to see Dannsair ever again. And that would be the worst punishment of all.

It was too much to risk.

I could barely stand waiting, but I had no choice. I learned the stablemaster's daily business and knew where to look for him. I sometimes spied on him in the marketplace as he bought fruit and hazelnuts. I watched him cross the green to the tall paling that confined my filly. The guard always opened the gate for him as he got near. He was courteous to the people he dealt with, but he rarely smiled.

Every time I saw him, I tried to gather my courage to approach him. I was scared to try, and that is the truth. Everything depended on his reaction. Everything.

So every time I saw him, I only stood, staring, my heart aching. I had come so far and waited so long. I had gotten inside the North Gate and worked so hard. And still, I had not been able to touch my filly, had not been able to put my arms around her neck and hug her. It was Old Brigit who saved me. She was gray-haired and wrinkled, but her eyes and her mind were clear as a girl's. She shared a name with the sweetest natured of saints, and if I had not met her, I would probably still be watching my filly from a distance.

CHAPTER SIX

I am being allowed to gallop more often. I hate the straps around my face. My mother never dragged me along on a rope. We walked together, most often, side by side. But it is joy to run in the fresh air, and I am grateful, even when it means straps and ropes.

Searching for work to earn my daily bread one rainy morning, I followed the scent of bitters and mordants. I knew the smell of a steaming dye pot from my mother's work at home.

I tapped on her door, and she opened it, took one look at my thin face, and brought me in to feed me. Her house was big, with dried rushes scattered in a thick layer on the dirt floor. The house was full of threaded looms. There were three small hearths for her dye pots.

She needed a lot of help, she said as I ate. She

wove on special looms; several were of a kind I had never seen before. She could weave fabric, woolen and flaxen, heavy and light. She could make anything, but her specialty was something I had never seen before. She made woven saddles—thick blankets shaped to fit a horse's back. And they were beautiful, patterned in many colors.

Irishmen often rode without a saddle of cloth or leather; Normans rarely did. Old Brigit had stopped weaving cloaks and leinte and had learned to weave Norman saddles.

She was Irish, but none of her customers cared—it was her work they loved. She sold every saddle she made to the Normans of Athenry, and every buyer I saw was very happy to give her his coins. She did beautiful work.

"You know something of dyeing?" she asked that first day.

"I do," I told her.

She smiled. "Then truly the faeries have brought you to my door, lad. I have noticed you here and there, looking hungry. If you will work hard, we can fix that."

I nodded, excited. The first few days, I

pounded woad leaves and madder root into powder fine enough to make the dye baths. I ground alum stone and iron to make her the mordants. And when it was time to stir the water-logged, heavy fabric, I did it.

My mother had taught me that the mordant—which is what makes the dye bind to the thread—is more important than whatever color recipes the dyer uses. No color is beautiful if it washes out of the cloth.

"Where did you learn so much, Trian?" Brigit asked me. "Mothers don't usually teach their sons to dye cloth."

I had gotten used to responding to my brother's name without an awkward pause each time, but the question itself gave me pause. I didn't know what to say.

My mother and the women of my tuath believed the presence of a man ruined the colors. My mother often waited until my father was gone on some journey or other to do her dyeing.

"She just needed help, I guess," I said after far too long a pause.

"Well, I think the tales about dyeing and men

are nonsense," she said firmly. "There is no law that says a boy can't dye cloth for his craft."

I nodded, but I was uncomfortable. I hated lying to her. She was the kindest person I had ever known. My mother would love her if they ever met, I was sure.

As the days passed, Old Brigit and I made good companions. Freed from having to search for work every day, I felt rich with time. She let me sleep inside her house from the first night onward. She made me a pallet of straw and rushes, and Cormac's cloak served as my blanket. It was wonderful to be warm and dry and safe. *Wonderful*.

Old Brigit had been lonely for years, I think, ever since her husband had died. She told me she missed him every day of the world. Whatever her reasons were, she took me into her household and I was more grateful than I could say. Being with her made me miss my family less. It eased my heart and my mind.

I did what I could to thank her. Like any member of any Irish family, I worked all day, every day, to earn my keep. Old Brigit had a cow named A Chara, and she was, as her name said, dear. Tame and good-natured, she needed no spancel to hold her still while I milked, and she gave enough to fill a big oaken bucket every day. I made cheese with every drop of milk we didn't drink.

Once milking was done, I found other chores. I dug drainage ditches to keep the season's rains from flooding Old Brigit's chicken byre. When I cleaned the stall where A Chara was kept, I piled the manure and dirty straw carefully so it would be easy to gather for the gardens the following spring. I pounded her barks and roots into dye powder, and I sat with her by her fire in comfortable silence every evening.

"Look at this," she said one day, leading me to a wooden trunk in the corner of the room. She opened the creaking lid and unwrapped a beautiful blue-green gown. "From my wedding day," she told me, smiling. She lifted out the dress and held it to her body, and I saw the shine of memories in her eyes. She placed a fragile lace hood over her hair, then took it off, her eyes distant and soft.

Back home, Old Orlaith often had the same

dreamy expression as she remembered back to the years of her youth. She was at least forty years old, with few years left to live. I hoped I would see her again before she passed away.

"We married in the church proper and all," Brigit said, stroking the fabric of the dress.

I nodded. My own parents had not—but then we lived a long way from any church.

"I was a widow five years after the wedding," Old Brigit said, her eyes shadowed. "We never had a family, and I never wanted another man." She gestured at her looms, her dye pots. "I suppose I have given my life to my craft."

Old Brigit was a fine dyer. I learned a great deal from her and couldn't wait to tell my mother. As I worked with her, I was surprised to see that Brigit did not only dye ells of cloth, as my mother did. She often dyed the thread before she wove it.

I cannot tell you why this had never occurred to me—that thread could be dyed before it was woven into cloth, but it had not. I wondered if my mother had ever thought of it. No one in our tuath had ever tried it.

Helping Brigit, I learned how to dye spun

thread. It was not too different from dyeing cloth, but evenness of color was harder to achieve. The difficulty lay with getting the dye to soak all the way into each thread. We had to wind it around squares of applewood—not too tightly or too loosely—so that it soaked through in the dye pot. Too tight, there were places left white. Too loose and it tangled in the pot.

Once it was dried near the fire, we would rewind it into skeins. On Brigit's looms, the blue threads were woven across the green ones, then both crossed a red stripe or a yellow one, then there might be a black stripe—and it all made a glorious pattern of colors crossing one another beyond anything I had ever imagined.

The first time I went into Brigit's workroom and saw her working on what she called the plaided cloth, I immediately wished that I could show it to my mother—which made me home-sick. I had been away from home nearly a full year now.

"Would you like to learn?" Brigit asked me one day.

I looked at her. "To weave?"

She nodded.

"I have no money to pay you for apprenticeship," I said.

She smiled. "I do not need payment. Would you like to learn?"

"Yes," I answered her. "Oh yes."

"Choose something that you would like to make," she said. "Perhaps a woolen brat to keep you warm for what remains of Gam?"

"I cannot pay for the wool," I said. "Unless you will trade me for more work of some kind."

She smiled. "You already work far more than you eat, Trian. What is it you wish to make?"

"I am not sure," I said, afraid to speak my true wish.

She was weaving an especially beautiful saddle for a Norman man. It was woolen, thick and soft, the front edge woven triple thick, then rolled back to make a pad to protect the horse's withers and back. There would be a soft flaxen cinch stitched on, and, of course, Norman iron-ring stirrups.

I sighed. From the first time she had shown it to me, I had longed to make one for Dannsair, for the day I would ride her—but I knew it would take years to learn.

Brigit simply looked at me, waiting for me to answer. When I did not, she turned back to her work. "Think about it, Trian, and tell me later. For now, will you build the fire beneath the iron kettle? I am going to grind and boil some woad."

I heard the steady thudding of the smooth stone in her hand begin. Her palms were callused and her fingers had become misshapen from years of pounding bark and leaves into dye powders, years of threading her looms. She began to hum in rhythm with her work.

"A belt," I said, and heard her humming stop.

"Tomorrow," she answered.

Brigit often let half a day pass without saying five words to me. Her silence was comfortable and kind. She reminded me so much of my mother in that way that it made me smile.

"When you want something from the faeries, from the saints, from life," she said quietly one day, "you must work hard to get it."

I looked at her.

"Whatever it is you are hiding," she said.

"Whatever it is that you would rather be doing when you are sorting thread for me. If there is some other craft that you want to learn—"

"I love horses," I said, without knowing I would say it. "I want to help care for them, to train them."

She smiled encouragement.

"I want to ask the stablemaster for work, but I am afraid to," I told her, the words leaking from my heart and into my mouth before I could stop them. "But my leine is so rough, and I know he and the baron hate beggars and—"

Old Brigit waved her hands to stop me. "If it is a new tunic you want," she said, "you are standing in the right place."

I had sounded like I was asking her a favor. "I didn't mean—" I began, but she hushed me a second time.

"You need a new leine. I will make you one."

"I will work so hard that you won't have to do anything to keep your house in order," I promised.

She laughed aloud. "You may start now, Trian, if you are ready," she said. She held out her pounding stone. "The finer the better." I nodded and set to work.

Not long after that the rains settled in, and Gam's constant chill kept most of Athenry's people hovering around their hearth fires for the coldest part of the winter. I was so grateful to Brigit for sharing her home with me.

She did make a leine, and it was perfect for my height—if I had really been a boy. It felt very strange to put it on. She taught me to weave a good belt. It was done with stiff squares of wood with a hole drilled in each corner for the thread to pass through. Turning the tablets changed the order of the threads that passed through them and made patterns as I wove. I chose a deep brown and the natural cream color of the wool with a little yellow in the borders. When it was finished, I asked Old Brigit what she thought.

She stopped her weaving and stood up to look at me. "You are a handsome boy, and the belt suits you very well."

I liked her so much and she had been so kind to me that I just wanted to tell her the truth. But I didn't dare.

I had less time to watch for Dannsair being taken out for her gallops because I was working hard for Brigit. But because of the cold weather, the horses were kept in more, too, so there were fewer chances anyway.

As the Feast of Imbolc drew closer, Brigit worked on the saddle. It was absolutely beautiful, crafted perfectly, with a woven fringe and tassels that would swing when the horse moved.

Old Brigit knew a leather tanner who made the stirrups in trade for an ell of cloth. I watched her fasten them on the saddle with long strips of leather that laced between the layers of her weaving. She began to weave the cinch on a special loom that had been made for the heaviest flax threads.

The winter days dragged past, and A Chara's milk thinned and slowed until we were mostly eating the cheese I had made before summer's end. Old Brigit said I saved her a half year's debt, making that cheese. She did not have to buy meat until five days before the Feast of Imbolc—when we would celebrate the beginning of spring.

"Will you deliver this for me?" Brigit asked

one morning during a lull in a storm. "Now, I mean, before the rain comes down hard again?"

"I would be pleased to," I told her. Lifting the saddle she had made, seeing close up the fineness of her work, made me smile. "Who is it for?" I asked her.

She smiled at me and tilted her head. "For the stablemaster. It is an Imbolc gift for his daughter. Cover it with your cloak against the sprinkling."

I looked down at the finished blanket, then met her eyes. "His daughter?"

She nodded. "Yes. The Norman girls sometimes ride, and this one has her own pony."

"But the stablemaster is—"

"He will be at the stables now, Trian," Brigit said, smiling. "Wear your new leine and belt. You can tell the guard I sent you."

CHAPTER SEVEN

❧ ❧ ❧

The darkness of this place is harder and harder to bear.
Only when I am allowed to run do I feel alive.

My knees were shaking, I tell you true, and 'it was not from the chill and damp. I fastened the little gold horse pin inside my leine for luck. Then I used my cloak to wrap the beautifully woven saddle and let the drizzle soak through my short hair and my new leine.

My hair had grown just long enough to drip down the back of my neck like a duck's tail, and so it did as I walked to the south end of the town. I kept going, across the wide meadow, then on to the tall paling fence that hid the stables.

"I have a newly made saddle for the stable-master," I told the guard.

"From Old Brigit?" he asked.

I nodded.

He swung the great paling gate inward and jerked his chin. "First barn, I think. If not, ask one of the boys."

I nodded, trembling more from nerves than the chilly rain.

I walked through the first barn slowly, looking into every stall even though I heard no voices. The barn was enormous. I did not count the stalls that day, but later I did. There were forty horses under that one roof, all of them sleek and healthy.

The stalls were on both sides of a wide aisle, as they had been at Conall's barn. I walked slowly. I wanted to find the stablemaster, of course, but more than that, more than *anything*, I wanted to see my beautiful Dannsair. It had taken me so long to get to this place, so long to get inside the North Gate, and a whole winter of working for Brigit to have a way to pass the stable guard...

Halfway down on the right side, I found her. I set down the cloak-wrapped saddle and stood at her stall gate. She looked at me quietly until I whispered her name. Then she came eagerly to the stall gate and reached over the planks to nuzzle my hair. She seemed to like it short. She snuffled, her nostrils wide. Her breath was warm.

"Dannsair," I said, my throat as tight as though someone were choking me. "I have missed you so much." She lowered her head and pushed at my chest.

"What are you doing there, boy?"

It was a man's voice, and I turned to see the stablemaster staring at me.

"I asked you a question. I don't know you. Do you have business here?"

"I do, sir," I managed. Then Dannsair whinnied, upset that I had stepped away from her. She struck at the planking with a forehoof and shook her head, her mane tossing. Her mane was longer now—and she was much taller.

The stablemaster was walking toward me, a stern look on his face. "Get away from that stall."

Dannsair was pacing. She wanted to follow me.

"I brought your daughter's saddle from Old Brigit, sir," I told the stablemaster. I lifted it free from the cloak and held it out for him to see. He examined it, his stern expression easing. Then he actually smiled. "Please tell the old woman that it is excellent crafting, as always." He ran his fingers over the thick roll at the front that would protect a horse's withers.

While he was looking at the intricate stitching I had watched Old Brigit labor over, I stepped backward and felt Dannsair's warm breath on the back of my neck.

"Get away," the man said, suddenly noticing me. "That filly is of rare blood, high-strung and dangerous."

I had no idea what to say to that. Dannsair? Dangerous? It wasn't possible. I reached up to touch her neck. She *was* taller. She tilted her head to nuzzle my neck.

"Did you feed her an apple?" the stablemaster demanded.

I shook my head, trembling. The last thing I wanted was to make this man angry with me. "No, sir. She whinnied when I walked past looking for you, sir, so I patted her."

He watched me run my hand down Dannsair's

shoulder. She half reared, whirled away, then trotted back to the stall gate, her neck arched. She wanted to play.

"I was hoping that you might give me work here in the stables, sir," I said. My voice shook a little, but if he noticed it, he gave no sign. "I am very good with horses, sir."

"Walk across the aisle and pat the bay mare on that side," he instructed me.

I could not imagine why he was asking me to do something so simple, but I did what I was told. The mare was heavy with foal, and I approached her slowly, talking quietly. Very few horsemen let their mares breed to foal before spring—it was a good thing she had this fine stable to shelter her from storms.

The mare was curious enough to walk to the front of her stall and put her head over the rail. Then, for some reason, her ears flickered backward, and I saw her eyes harden with suspicion. Perhaps she had been treated cruelly by someone. In any case, I took the hint and stepped back just before she snapped at me. Had I not moved, she might have had my right ear between her teeth.

"I am not sure she will let me touch her, sir," I said. "Not without a few days of convincing her she can trust me. I will try again if you want me to," I added, in case he thought I was a coward. I stood taller and met his eyes directly.

He nodded. "I can use a boy who knows how not to get kicked while he cleans stalls."

"I know horses, sir," I said. I thought about telling him that I knew how to help foaling mares, too, but I didn't. Conall had not believed me.

"Can you ride?"

The question turned me around to face him. "Yes," I said, though it was really not true.

At home, I had often sat on Dannsair's mother's back when she was inside the great earthen walls of our rath. The sweet-natured gray mare would then walk, slowly, grazing while I talked to her quietly. But I had never tried to ride any horse at a trot or a gallop.

"A little," I added, after such a long pause that the stablemaster laughed.

"Come at daybreak tomorrow."

"I will, sir," I said, but he was already gesturing for me to leave.

It was pouring rain when I stepped out of the barn, and I slid my cape over my shoulders. I walked in the cold rain back to Old Brigit's house, my bare feet sinking in the mud—and I was smiling all the way.

"He asked me to tell you the saddle is beautiful," I told her as I stepped in the door. "Very well crafted. He seemed very pleased with it."

She nodded and smiled. "Did you ask about work?"

I grinned. "I did. I am to come first thing in the morning." I shook the rain out of my cloak and scraped most of the mud off my feet. Then I went in.

"I will still help you," I promised. "And whatever pay I make, I will give to you."

She patted my cheek and looked into my eyes. "I need no payment beyond your work, Trian." She smiled. "The day I was told I could learn to weave, I was so happy. It seemed like magic to me then. It still does. I was born to weave."

I nodded. I knew exactly what she meant—and I knew that she could see inside my heart. I felt the same way.

There was something about being around horses that made me feel happier than I felt anywhere else. I had been born to work with them, and I had been born to be Dannsair's foster mother—and her friend.

That evening, after our evening bowl of boiled oats, Brigit lit three tallow candles. By their light, she showed me how to weave a fancy braid that made a round cord of great strength. As always, she was patient with my mistakes.

Later, when I was on my pallet, the room dark as midnight, I could hear Old Brigit's steady breathing. I was so grateful to her. I smiled in the darkness. After all my worry and all my work, I was going to see Dannsair every day. Every day! I would be able to make sure she was cared for, that she knew I was close, and that I would keep her safe.

It was the best gift anyone could ever receive.

I tell you true, it made my heart dance.

CHAPTER EIGHT

❧ ❧ ❧

My mother has come at last. She has not yet taken me out
of the dark place, but she will. She always has.

*C*leaning stalls is hard, unlovely work.
I wore my old leine to keep my new one
clean, and every day I went to the stable singing.

I sang as I worked and smiled when I saw the
stablemaster nod his approval when he inspected
the stalls to make sure I was doing a good job.

I was careful not to let anyone see me paying
special attention to Dannsair. I didn't want to call
attention to how close we were, how much she
trusted me. Whenever I cleaned her stall, she

wheeled in tight circles, half rearing and tossing her head.

I was not the only stable boy, of course. There were two big barns standing side by side behind the paling, so more help was needed. There were several grooms who combed out manes and tails and rubbed shedding hair from the horses' coats with braided straw whisks and rough cloth.

There were four boys who fed, measuring out the pecks of oats and corn and fetching water in buckets. They were done by noon, most days.

Mucking out stalls took longer than feeding.

There were three of us hired for the task, all arriving before sunrise—the other two were named Fothud and Guaire, the stablemaster told me.

They were not unhappy to see me. The boy I was replacing had been lazy. The stablemaster had finally caught him sleeping in the dried grass in the fodder byre, something he had often done while the other two did his share of the work.

They told me the pay was five silver pennies each full moon. I had never seen a silver penny from Galway, though I remembered my father once talking about de Burgo pennies. I couldn't wait to hold them in my hand, to be able to buy bread or apples or wheat meal for Old Brigit's larder. I would be able to go to market and come back with a haunch of venison so we could have boiled meat for a whole fortnight!

Guaire and Fothud led me around the barns my first day, showing me a narrow path that led to a walled field behind the buildings, small pens for mares in foal, and the byre filled with bins where oats and corn were kept.

They were friendly, and I liked them both. At noon, when they went out past the rock-walled field to relieve themselves, I had to lie and say I didn't need to go just then. Later, once we were all working again, I stole away and ran down the narrow path alone. It scared me, to work so closely with boys—what if one of them realized I was a girl? The Normans let their girls ride now and then, but I was sure that no girl, Irish or Norman, would be allowed to work in the barns.

None of us worked on the days of the Feast of Imbolc. That year, the first day of spring was fair and warm, which made everyone happy.

Imbolc was even more celebrated here among

the Normans than it had been at home with my tuath. Only the Normans didn't call it Imbolc. For the Baron of Athenry and the Normans in his court and in the town, spring began with the feast of Saint Brigid. She was part of our Feast of Imbolc—for the Normans, it was her day.

I had known about her all my life. Being around Normans in a town full of priests, I learned even more. She had been pure of heart, mind, and soul, and had loved cattle and the pure white milk they produced. Her kindness had been endless. There were so many stories about her healing sick women and purifying fouled wells—all manner of saintly acts.

The priests led prayers to Saint Brigid while the women cooked goose and eel and lamb. The odor of plentiful food hung over the paths of Athenry town.

I had seen people crossing at the ford of the Clareen for two or three days before, some of them coming to celebrate the saint's day with friends and family.

Irish and Norman alike, people wore their finest clothes as they walked the paths of the town on their way to family and friends. I saw some of the same girls I'd seen from my holly tree at the edge of the meadow. The one who had been worried about her mean cousin seemed much happier now. I saw her walking with the stable-master and a number of others, on their way to the priory for the churchmen's service. Was this his daughter? The one who would have Old Brigit's woven saddle for her gift today?

Most of the Irish people went to the priory as well. I did not. I had nothing fancy to wear, and I did not want any of them to notice me. Old Brigit was staying at home, too, and we decided to have our own little feast. We put on our best clothes and set about cooking.

"You are my own Saint Brigid," I told her.

She blushed. "Hush, Trian," she said. "I am no saint."

"You have been one to me, and I am grateful," I said, and I meant it.

"Are you grateful enough to go to market to buy us a little honey?" she asked, laughing. "It will be good in our milk pudding." She handed me a penny and I went out into the sunshine.

I saw Niall when I was halfway to the market square. We talked a moment, and I found his curiosity nettlesome as always.

"Where do you sleep now?" he wanted to know. I told him, and he nodded somberly. "I know Old Brigit. Everyone does. Did she make your new leine?"

"Yes." I glanced down at my clothes. Niall still made me uneasy. I glanced up and noticed the three Norman boys who loved to taunt me walking toward us.

I felt my stomach knot up.

It seemed to be my day to see everyone I usually tried to avoid. "I must hurry back," I told Niall, and was walking away before he could say good-bye. I was sorry to be rude to him, but I could not wait for the Norman boys to come any closer.

After that day, I was even more careful. If I was ever going to save Dannsair from becoming a warhorse, I had to keep my gender, my real self, my real purpose here, a secret. I hid inside Brigit's warm byre, spinning thread and stirring dye pots when I wasn't working in the stables.

The weather warmed, and it was soon time to

put away my cloak. Old Brigit gave me a sturdy linen bag for my things, and I wove a patterned band with my wooden tablet to tie it closed. Old Brigit kissed my forehead with great solemnity and told me that if I ever decided that I didn't want to spend my life with horses, I would make a good weaver.

I cannot tell you how proud that made me.

Every morning, I nodded politely at the boys who fed the horses but did not speak with them. My life of secrecy was becoming a habit.

Fothud and Guaire and I worked from dawn to dusk, but at first, I stayed away from them, too. I was so afraid that someone might guess that I wasn't a boy. That would be the cruelest fate of all—to have come this far and managed to be near Dannsair again, then have my being a girl ruin everything.

I knew I didn't look like a girl now. I had practiced standing with my shoulders squared, and speaking in my lowest voice until it was a habit. I said very little and often said nothing at all.

My old leine was truly tattered now, increasingly tight across my back, and well above my knees as I grew. I waited for Fothud and Guaire to tease me about it.

They didn't.

I tell you true, they were both good-hearted boys. They reminded me of my brothers, and of Bebinn's dear Tally.

The best part of my life was this: Every day I stole moments with Dannsair. I stayed at the barns later in the evening and came earlier in the morning than the others. When I was sure there was no one else in the barn, I would go into her stall and lean against her shoulder and talk to her the way I always had, telling her everything I hoped and everything I feared.

Dannsair's restlessness eased, but only a little. Guaire and Fothud still thought she was dangerous—and so did the boys who carried the oat buckets every morning. When anyone came close to her stall, she reared and pawed at the dirt.

When I cleaned it, she did the same thing, but I knew she wasn't mean or dangerous. She was desperate to play.

Dannsair had been free all day, every day, at Conall's barns. She had gotten used to following me through the forests to our creek, then to the meadows, and up the long hill to Gealach's pasture wall, galloping to catch me as I ran.

We had spent every day alone. I had taught her to come when I called her. She had learned to stay at a hand signal and waited for me to call her again before she moved. Now she only got out of her stall when one of the riders took her for a gallop—which had been less often as the weather worsened. Now that the air smelled of early spring, she wanted to be out more than ever.

And this cannot be forgotten: Dannsair's dam had passed on fine, rare bloodlines from the deserts that lay across the eastern sea. Her sire was a moon-colored stallion from Connaught's wilds, strong and proud as any stallion could be. My filly had inherited more spirit than most.

Dannsair hated being confined. I couldn't figure out what in the world I could do about it. I only knew that I had to think of something. If I could not, the stablemaster would soon be right— my beautiful Dannsair would be dangerous.

CHAPTER NINE

✷ ✷ ✷

*At last, my mother has let me out. I love to gallop
here in the dim light as she perches on my back.
It felt strange at first, but I like carrying her so
that we can go faster. She is very small.*

*A*s a fortnight of rainy days dragged past,
I began to talk a little more with Fothud
and Guaire. They were both very good with the
horses, kind and patient. They were kind to me,
too, in a quiet way, and they worked very hard.

We all liked going home a little early, so we
worked steadily. One day, without meaning
to, we fell into a kind of race, pitching the
soiled bedding into the aisle with our hay forks
in such a fury that we finished long before
usual, laughing and tired—and very glad to go

home when the sun was still warm and bright.

The day after that, Fothud came to me with a challenge. We would all race every other day. The two who lost would each do two of the winner's stalls on the alternate day—meaning the winner could go home earlier than the other two.

We usually started with Dannsair's barn simply because it was closest to the gate, then went on to the second barn. I was careful not to win at first so that when I finally did, neither of the boys resented me for it. After that, every time I won, I would pretend to leave, then I would go back into Dannsair's barn while Fothud and Guaire finished up.

Listening for the boys' voices, I would talk softly to Dannsair, rubbing her forehead and her neck, trying to calm her down if enough rainy weather had kept her in the barn for days on end.

One day I slid from the stall rails onto her back and sat quietly, talking as I had to her mother. She stood still, twitching her ears, curious about the weight on her back, but calm, trusting me completely.

After that, I often sat on her back. One day I

pushed at her neck, gently turning her head until she took a step in that direction.

That single step ignited all my old dreams of riding her. She was young, but she was very tall for her age—and I was small for my age and skinny as a stick, as Old Brigit often said. I knew I could never take Dannsair out of the stable without permission from the stablemaster—and that he would never give it—but my dreams blossomed inside that little stall.

Dannsair really was tall for a rising yearling. Her chest was deepening, and her legs were long. I had wondered whether she would be slender and swift like her mother, or heavily muscled and strong like her father. It appeared that she would be some of both—though it was too early to tell.

I had watched her sire, Gealach, for hours at a time back at Conall's barns. He was high-spirited to a fault, pacing and galloping constantly. Her mother had been calm, but maybe that had been because she was in foal. My mother had often said that a pregnant mare was no different from a pregnant woman—her spirits ran both high and low—and changed often.

One stormy evening, when I had won the stall-mucking race, I talked to Dannsair while Fothud and Guaire finished their work. Then I hid while they were leaving—and I was alone with Dannsair.

"What will we do?" I asked her. "It's just us, everyone else gone home for the night."

She whickered and bent to rub her ear on my arm. Then she snorted and danced backward, half rearing and shaking her mane.

I smiled. "Don't you wish we could just run away?"

She cantered a tight circle, then reared again. She pranced back to me, then stopped, her nostrils flared.

I rubbed her ears. She whickered and lowered her head, and I could feel her breath on my shoulder. Was there any place in all of Eire where there was no war, no warhorses, no one who would try to take her from me?

I sighed and watched Dannsair, restless and uneasy in the stall. She stamped her front hooves and turned, pacing, tossing her head.

"I wish I could take you out for a gallop." I said it wistfully. I knew it was entirely impossible. The guard at the door would never let me lead Dannsair past him. If he was asleep, as he often was by evening, her hoofbeats would wake him. Stall muckers were not allowed to take the horses out of the barns. I would never be allowed to come back.

I looked at the long barn aisle and remembered the aisle in Conall's barn. It had not been as long as this—and Dannsair had been much younger—but she had used it to gallop, to play during the worst weather.

I touched Dannsair's muzzle. "If I let you out, will you promise to stay calm?"

She ducked her head and it looked like she was nodding. I laughed quietly. "Do you remember the things I taught you?" This time she lifted her head and paced away from me, then back, switching her tail.

Knowing that if anything happened, I would lose my job at the stables and probably be forced to leave Athenry altogether and forever—still I rested my hand on the iron latch.

Dannsair was miserable, and it hurt me to watch her wearing a circular track in the earthen floor of her stall. When she saw my hand on the gate, she came forward, her eyes bright in the dimming afternoon light.

I could hear rain on the thatched roof overhead. It had turned rainy and chilly, and the ground was a bog of mud and brown puddles outside. Spring was slow in coming in spite of the passing of Imbolc. No horse had been led out for exercise in days.

I took a deep breath.

Then another.

Then I pushed the latch free. Dannsair nearly knocked me down as she came out. She lashed her tail back and forth across her own flanks, then broke into a canter. She went to the end of the aisle, then turned and came back, then did it again.

I counted each time she passed me. I got to forty before she slowed to a trot of her own will. Then we played. Dannsair remembered perfectly how to stay in one place when I asked her to. She came every time I called her name, too. She loved that game above any other because it meant more cantering.

It was odd to see her playing in her old way now that she was so tall. She would get heavier, I was sure, but she was already higher at the withers than most of the baron's horses—and she carried herself proudly, her neck arched. I thought she was by far the most beautiful horse in any of the baron's barns, of course, because I loved her. But I think it was true, too.

That evening, I was scared to have the guard notice me leaving late, worried that he would say something to the stablemaster. But he was asleep.

Rather than opening the creaking gate to let myself out, I walked a long way down the line of palings, then climbed over, jumping down on the far side. I skinned my shoulder that night, but I got better at it with practice.

After that night, I let Dannsair out every chance I got. Once she was calmer, I could not resist sitting on her in the stall a few moments before sliding off and opening the gate.

Then there came a night when I did what I had always longed to do. I undid the stall latch and went in, pulling the gate to, but not relatching it. I sat on Dannsair for a few moments, then, without allowing my mind to stop what was in my heart to do, I leaned out and pushed the gate open.

She turned, and with me sitting nervously on her back, she did what she always did as she came out of the stall gate. She half reared and sprang into a joyous canter. I barely managed to hang on as she went the length of the barn and plunged to a near stop in order to turn.

That was when I lost my balance and slid off, awkwardly, stumbling backward, as she pivoted to canter back the other way. Unable to keep my feet beneath me, I sat down hard. She stopped and trotted back to nuzzle me. I was rubbing my tailbone for a few days afterward.

I collected my silver pennies from the baron's clerk—a little man in a gold-threaded coat who wore a wide gold band on one forefinger. All the free Irish who worked for the baron had to line up in the market square to collect their pay. I saw Fothud and Guaire the first time, and we made an agreement to take turns coming early—the early one letting the other two in line when they arrived. As a result, none of us ever had to wait very long. That gave us time to look around in the market.

I loved the marketplace, with its baskets of apples and boxes of seaweed and herbs and meat. I loved the beautiful, tall cross of stone. Each time I was paid, I spent some of my pennies on good cheese and apples for Old Brigit's larder and tried to give her the rest. She always refused, so I put them by, hiding the coins under my pallet. I owed her a debt, and I was determined to find a way to repair it.

I worked hard in the barns, and I worked hard for Old Brigit, but the center of my life was Dannsair. Every time I rode her, I did better. On the second full moon after Imbolc, I rode her at a canter up the barn aisle, then stayed on perfectly as she skidded into her pivoting turn and cantered back.

It was wonderful.

I was so happy I sang all the way home.

The next day I asked Old Brigit for a bit of thick woolen cloth to use as a rag—I wanted to be able to rub Dannsair's coat smooth and shining after her runs. She gave me pieces of a worn old blanket and asked me no questions. Her eyes twinkled, and I was sure she knew I was keeping something to myself, coming home late most evenings. But she said no more, and I was grateful to her for that, on top of everything else.

I taught Dannsair to turn the way I wanted her to. It wasn't hard because she really only had two choices in the barn aisle. I just touched her neck and leaned to the side each time and praised her when she got it right.

I taught myself how to grip her mane and swing onto her back as I had seen my father and his men do many times. Dannsair quickly learned to brace herself against my weight and stood very still. I learned more slowly.

It is *much* harder than it looks. Dannsair was always kind—she nuzzled my hair when I sat up, rubbing my backside. Finally, I got good at it.

Dannsair learned to stop when I said the word *stay*—the same game we had played when she was a foal, only now I was on her back. We played our old game of her coming when I called her, too. It seemed to me that she could very nearly read my thoughts—and I could read hers.

Every night I kissed Dannsair's silky forehead as I left. Every moment I was not at the barns, I worked hard for Old Brigit. I spent almost all my silver pennies on food and goods for both of us. The stars shone in the sky and the days went past, each one longer than the last and each one warmer. And the year turned toward Beltaine and the beginning of summer.

Beltaine was always a joyous feast day in my tuath, coming as it did on the heels of the hungriest time of year. The cows were close to calving and would soon come into milk—so everyone knew there would soon be cheese and cream and curds to eat again.

As the weather truly turned, the riders began taking the young horses out to gallop again almost every day. I began coming home early more often to help Old Brigit with whatever she was doing. I knew I could never repay her kindness, but I was determined to try.

I began braiding a bridle, using heavy linen thread that Brigit gave me, working it into round braided cords. I tried to pay her for the thread, but she refused, as usual. So I bought her a new milking stool—her old one was cracked.

I kept the braided straps tight and strong. I knew that if I ever got to use it, it would have to be strong—to match Dannsair's spirit.

"In case I ever own a horse," I told Old Brigit when she noticed what I was making.

"And you will, Trian," she said firmly. "Perhaps many horses. There are men who make a craft of horse breeding."

I nodded, feeling a stab of envy. Men did, yes. But not women. I hid the finished bridle in a woven flax bag Old Brigit had given me for my things. It already held the water flask and cloak that Cormac had given me, the remaining length of yellow cloth from an old brat that had belonged to my mother, and of course, the little gold horse pin, still fastened to the new leine Old Brigit had made for me.

When I put the bag away, I hugged it to my chest for a moment. My family's past was in it—as were all my dreams for the future.

CHAPTER TEN

I will carry my mother, who is kind to me.
She sits still so that I may move easily.
And she does not hurt me. She has never hurt me.

I was mucking out stalls in Dannsair's barn one morning when the stablemaster and two other men came into the barn.

One of the men was tall and thin, and the other was stout and gray-haired. The thin man said very little. The heavyset man seemed to talk a great deal—but in a low, deep voice that didn't carry.

I watched and listened as well as I could without *seeming* to. The stablemaster was happy with my work, and I didn't want to do *anything* to change his opinion. I could not stand the idea of being separated from Dannsair again.

Not ever.

"This one, perhaps," I heard the stablemaster say. I glanced up. They had stopped in front of a stall that held a tall sorrel mare.

"You have a fortnight to select the horses and prepare them?" the thin man asked.

The stablemaster nodded. "The race will be held on the Feast of Beltaine." He cleared his throat. "Any two horses, any age, any size—but only two entries for each owner, Irish or Norman."

"Irish?" the stout man demanded. "De Burgo has invited the Irish to race? Why?"

The stablemaster didn't answer him except to shrug, clear his throat again, and spit into the straw.

They passed me without so much as a nod from any of them. I kept my head down as they went by. I kept working—and listening.

"We have all heard about this one," the stout man said after a long moment. "Her dam was the desert mare that was lost, and the sire is Gealach? That Irish rí…what is his name?"

"McDonagh," the stablemaster said.

The man nodded. "McDonagh will be sorry he traded her off. She is a beauty."

My heart stood still. I half turned so I could see them standing in front of Dannsair's stall. She had moved to the back to be as far away from them as possible. She nickered, calling *me*. But I could not go to her—not without letting the stablemaster see how much she trusted me. If he knew how much I had been training her . . .

"She is extraordinary," the thin man said, interrupting my thoughts. "Rising two?"

"No. She's just a yearling, but she's big and heavy-boned for her age," the stablemaster said.

I gripped the long oak handle of the hay fork. Why were they looking at Dannsair?

"She is very well muscled for a yearling," the stout man said. "Do you work her that hard, even at this age?"

I kept at my work, but blindly, jabbing my oaken hay fork at the soiled straw without really seeing it. All the nights of cantering back and forth, kicking and rearing—if Dannsair was muscled, it was from playing with me.

I glanced up to see the stablemaster shake his

head, then shrug. "She is led at gallop when weather permits. No more than the others."

You know," the thin man said, "fit as she is, she could manage the course."

"Is she as fast as she looks?" the stout man asked.

"The exercise boy says she pulls ahead easily when he gallops her, that she nearly drags him along," the stablemaster said. "No one has ever ridden her, though, she's half wild."

I glanced down the aisle; the thin man was opening Dannsair's stall. She was still pressed against the back wall, but he didn't try to get any closer to her. He glanced at the stablemaster over his shoulder. "The baron demands a win?"

I saw the stablemaster nod. "At all costs," he said. "It's de Burgo taunting him by inviting the Irish to enter. The baron will not lose to an Irishman's horse."

The thin man shrugged and came back through the stall gate. "If she were mine, I'd see if she would carry a light rider—do you have a boy who could handle her?"

The stablemaster shook his head. "What boy could handle her?"

No one answered him.

They stopped in front of three more stalls as they walked back up the aisle.

I stood still after they had gone, simply forcing myself to breathe. I had not expected this—or at least, not this soon.

Most likely, I thought, reasoning with myself, the stablemaster would choose other horses for this race. Dannsair was fast and full of promise, but she was very young—and he would not find a boy who could ride her.

Dannsair barely let the exercise boy handle her—and she only allowed that because she had learned that he led her out of her stall and gave her a chance to run. I wished, for the thousandth time, that I could be the one to lead her out into the sunshine, just to see her truly gallop.

Back home, my father, because he was the rí of our tuath, sometimes challenged other tuatha to bring their fastest mounts to race. The men often placed wagers on the races, of course, with my father witnessing the bets to ensure that no one cheated.

Bebinn, Gerroc, and I had always watched the

races from the little hill above our rath. I loved seeing the horses coming up the long, gentle rise to the finish line. As they came closer, we could hear their sobbing breath—then our cheering would rise until all anyone could hear was excited shouts and hoofbeats.

All these thoughts made me smile, made me homesick, then, abruptly, I remembered the scream of a bay colt when I was five or six years old. He had caught one front hoof in a tangle of brambles. He fell, breaking the bones in his cannon and pastern. The rider had managed to leap clear. But the horse...

Gerroc's father had owned him—and had had to kill him to end his pain.

My whole body jerked in revulsion at that terrible memory, and I dropped the stable fork. Its oaken handle clattered against the stall rails.

I stood still, breathing hard.

I could not let Dannsair's life be wasted like that. I could not allow her to be hurt. If the stable-master chose her to race, we would have to escape, one way or another.

CHAPTER ELEVEN

⚘ ⚘ ⚘

My mother was very sorry for the bitter-tasting
thing, for the pain. She will make sure it
does not happen again if she can.

The next morning, just as the sun was rising, I ran through the maze of paths between the houses and byres of Athenry town. I kept running all the way to the stables, crossing the wide green field with long strides.

Fothud and Guaire were not long behind me, and we set about work as usual. I was nearly half finished with my share when I heard voices.

I looked up. The stablemaster was coming into the barn, this time trailed by two Norman boys. He led them straight to Dannsair's stall, and it was only as he passed me that I saw he had a bridle in his hand. I stared at the boys. They were about my age, no more, slim and light. Oh no, oh no. I prayed to the old gods, the faeries, and Saint Brigid—and I pretended to work.

"Trian," the stablemaster called. "Come here for a moment."

Wary, I came out of the gate. Both boys frowned at me. I caught my breath. I recognized one of them. As I got closer, he smiled, a thin-lipped insult of a smile. It was one of the boys who always taunted me.

"The filly is used to Trian," the stablemaster said to the boys, motioning me closer. He handed me the bridle. I looked down at the heavy bit, knowing what he would say next.

"See if you can get this on her."

"She will fight the bit," I said.

He frowned. "Do as you are told."

I took the bridle from him, staring at the finger-size bar of iron. "She would do better without it," I said as quietly as I could.

The stablemaster lifted one hand. "Do you dare argue with me?"

I saw the Norman boy smile again. He was enjoying this. Helpless to do anything but obey the stablemaster, I stepped forward. If he was determined to put a bridle on Dannsair, I couldn't stop him—and if I did it, I could at least be sure that it was done gently.

Dannsair was trembling at the back of her stall. I walked toward her, talking to her very quietly. I had seen my father and Conall and a dozen other men put a bitted bridle on a horse, so I knew how it was done. But would Dannsair let me?

Dannsair's ears came forward when she recognized me, and she came toward me, her head high enough to keep an eye on the stablemaster and the two boys.

The moment I was close enough, Dannsair nuzzled my face. When I lifted the bridle, she sniffed at it for a moment, then began nibbling at my hair.

"This is important," I whispered to her, stepping back to lift the bridle again so she would look at it. I rubbed it along her jaw and neck, then let her smell it once more.

I took a deep breath and lifted the bit and

touched it to her lips, gently sliding my hand down her jaw, easing my thumb into the natural gap between her front and back teeth. She loosened her jaw to lick my thumb, and I carefully worked the bit into her mouth.

Dannsair lifted her head sharply when she felt the cool iron bar lying against her tongue, but I kept talking, holding the bit in place until she brought her head down far enough for me to slide the headstall over her ears. I reknotted the straps to fit her. Then I stood back to pat Dannsair's neck as she worked her tongue beneath the cold iron, shaking her head uneasily. I patted her and praised her, and she rubbed her cheek against my shoulder.

"Well done," the stablemaster said. I turned. He had opened the stall gate wide and was holding his hand out for the reins.

"I will walk her for you if you like, sir," I said, hoping he wouldn't get angry. I was desperate to stay with Dannsair.

He nodded curtly. "Just keep her calm." Then he started off, followed by the boys. Dannsair and I came last. I kept wishing that I could just get on her and ride away. I thought about it, but knew it wouldn't work for the same reason it had always been impossible. Unless we got a long way from the castle without anyone knowing, the baron's men would find us.

The stablemaster led the way out, then turned away from the paling fence where the guard stood and followed the narrow path between the buildings. Coming out the other side, he made his way toward the walled meadow behind the barns.

Once we were inside it, he lifted the boy who had taunted me onto Dannsair's back. I held my breath, wishing she would throw him, but hoping she would not. I didn't want her whipped.

Dannsair was puzzled, but she stood still as the stablemaster held the reins for a moment. Then he stood back.

"Start slowly," he said to the boy. "See if you can get her to respond to your heels and the bridle."

The boy nodded, then glanced at me. Then, like a fool, he kicked hard at Dannsair's sides, startling her. When she jumped, he lost his balance and slid sideways. He used the reins to right himself, wrenching her head around and clamping the bit down over her tongue. She squealed and reared in surprise and pain.

"Loosen the reins," the stablemaster shouted at the boy. "Just let her run." But by then it was too late. Dannsair was terrified. She obeyed her instincts and tried to gallop away from trouble and pain, but the boy clung to her mane, still jerking the reins.

"He's hurting her!" I screamed.

If he heard me, he gave no sign of it. Dannsair reared again, frantic to escape the pain of the steel bar in her mouth. The boy was too off-balance, too scared, to realize what he was doing.

Dannsair lowered her head and took off, galloping flat out toward the wall on the far side of the big pasture. There, she slid to a halt, half reared, and pivoted to gallop back.

The stablemaster shouted for the boy to hold on, but he could not. It was the pivot that threw him. He lost his seat and slewed sideways, one hand jerking the reins, the other buried in Dannsair's mane.

The pain of the bit, having the boy's weight all to one side, and his hands tearing at her mane was too much for Dannsair. She reared, came down hard, then leaped sideways, twisting in the air, landing with her forefeet first, the impact dislodging the boy from her back entirely.

He hit the ground hard and lay still for a few seconds before he stirred and sat up. What he did after that, I can't tell you. I was watching my Dannsair galloping onward from where the boy fell, her mane streaming out behind her.

She raced across the pasture, her stride lengthening. I waited for her to slide to a stop and pivot to gallop back toward me. She did not. Instead, at the far end, she gathered herself, timed her stride perfectly, and leaped, sailing over the pasture wall, galloping away on the far side.

The stablemaster shouted at the boy, then ran back to the barns. Dannsair was still cantering away from me, headed toward the open field between the barns and the town of Athenry—the field I crossed every morning.

I ran after Dannsair and climbed over the pasture wall, bruising one knee badly. I stumbled, but kept upright and kept running. I could still see Dannsair. She was enjoying her sudden freedom, shaking her head to try to get rid of the hateful bit in her mouth.

I heard the stablemaster shouting, and I glanced back toward the barns. The Norman boy, the stable guard, and Guaire and Fothud ran along behind him, headed toward the front gate of the stables.

Dannsair had veered to run beside the town wall. It took me a moment to understand what she was doing. The town wall was higher than her head—there was no chance of her jumping it. But she could see the North Gate standing wide open at the other end of the huge enclosure that surrounded Athenry town and its castle. And she could see the forest beyond it.

The gate was open because a line of merchant carts was coming in. The baron's guards were facing outward, not inward. They clearly assumed the sound of hoofbeats was from a horse being ridden, not one trying to escape, because not one of them turned to look.

Dannsair was past them in an eyeblink, making the cart drivers shout and curse as she startled their donkeys.

I ran faster, knowing it was hopeless. Dannsair was through the gate, galloping outside the town walls before I was even halfway to the gate. I staggered to a stop and watched, nearly blinded by my own tears.

Glancing over my shoulder, I saw the stablemaster running back toward the barns, the boys strung out behind him. I was sure he was cursing himself for not taking the time to bridle and mount a horse when he'd come through the barns the first time. If he had, he could have galloped after Dannsair. Now, we might never catch her. I stared after him, feeling helpless.

Then, looking back toward Dannair, I saw a miracle. Guided by chance, the grace of Saint Brigid, the kindness of the faeries, or her own memories of happier gallops, Dannsair had not run straight into the forest. She had gone out the gates and turned right, galloping the route where she was often led for exercise. That meant she would come back along the outside of the wall not far from where I stood before she turned uphill.

Desperation made my feet light as I whirled

and ran straight for the town wall. I had never run that fast in my life, but the wall itself nearly stopped me. It was much higher than the pasture wall. I had only little ledges and chinks in the stone to use as I struggled upward. I managed to throw one arm over the top and scrambled over, falling more than jumping to the ground.

Bruised, my hands and feet bleeding, I stumbled upright. Dannsair had already gone past. She was galloping at an angle, headed uphill toward the path that ran through the woods.

"Dannsair!" I shouted. "Dannsair!"

She flicked her ears and her pace slowed.

"Dannsair!"

She slowed again, turning in a long circle to head back toward me. There was blood on her jaw—the bit had cut her. But she was calming down, and as she had done a thousand times before, she cantered to me and stopped.

I put my arms around her neck and cried, leaning against her. Then, hands shaking, I took the bridle off. And there I stood a moment later when the stablemaster galloped up. There were four of the baron's guardsmen with him, and they positioned their mounts in a loose circle around Dannsair.

"Get the bridle back on her," the stablemaster said.

I shook my head. "Her mouth is cut and bruised. I don't need it."

He scowled at me. He was about to order the men to take Dannsair from me, I was sure. Before he could, I locked my left hand in Dannsair's mane and swung up. I heard them all draw in a quick breath. "She is exhausted and scared," I said as calmly as I could. "May I take her back to the barn now, sir?"

The stablemaster nodded, keeping his face stern, as though he had known all along that I could ride Dannsair. I touched her neck gently, and she turned and started off at a walk. And that is the way we all went back into Athenry, Dannsair and I leading the way.

CHAPTER TWELVE

✖ ✖ ✖

My mouth is sore, and I am back in the dark place.
I only hope my mother comes soon and that
she will stay close. The others scare me.

*T*he next morning, the stablemaster met me at the stables gate. Since he didn't know I had been listening, he explained everything to me, then he said I could ride Dannsair in the race if I could prove I could handle her.

My heart hammered inside my body, and I tried to think. I had thought he would give up on entering Dannsair. But if he didn't, if I was the one riding her, I could make sure she didn't get hurt, whether or not she won.

"There will be a prize for the winning rider,"

he said. "A generous prize. Gold and silver coins."

That had not occurred to me.

"Would the prize be enough for me to buy Dannsair?" I asked him, then realized my mistake.

He frowned. "Dannsair?"

I bit my lip, then told the truth. "I call the filly that."

"Dannsair," he said, then nodded. "I have heard worse names for horses."

"Would the prize be enough?" I asked again.

He looked at me, then nodded slowly. "Perhaps. I will ask the baron." Then he started walking, talking as he went. "Have you ridden a horse without a saddle before?"

I ran to catching up, nodding, glad he had not asked the reverse. I had never ridden *with* one.

"Good. If you can do without it, it's that much less weight. Bridle her. We can begin this morning."

"She doesn't need a bridle," I said, then caught myself a second time.

For five or six long heartbeats, he just looked into my eyes. Then he spoke. "Have you been riding her? Where? Do not lie to me."

I hesitated. "She was so restless and lonely and...so was I—" I stopped and felt my face flush. It was truer than I cared to admit.

For the first time, the stablemaster's face softened.

"I meant no harm," I said, squaring my shoulders and meeting his eyes.

He exhaled and rubbed his chin. "I believe you. And you may have done me a great favor," he said. "Tell me true. How much have you ridden her?"

I explained.

"Never out of the barn?"

I shook my head.

"Without a bridle?"

I nodded.

He stood aside. "Lead her out. Show me."

Dannsair came out calmly when I opened the gate. I swung up and cantered her to the end of the aisle. She slid to a halt, then pivoted as she always did, to the right this time, since I had touched that side of her neck. And we cantered back.

The stablemaster's brows were arched as I rode Dannsair back toward him. "Stay," I said, and Dannsair stopped.

The stablemaster looked as though I had handed him a present. "If you can win this race," he said slowly, "the baron will be very happy. And the prize will be yours." He looked at Dannsair. "She can do it, I think."

I waited until he met my eyes again. "The only reward I want is to own the filly."

"I will ask the baron this evening," he said.

I smiled, feeling half sick with relief, hope, and caution. I would ride her in the race, not some fool boy who would break her leg trying to win, and there was a chance that winning would make her mine. If the baron agreed to take the prize as payment. *If.*

The stablemaster extended the bridle again. "Put it on. I want to take her out."

"She hates the bit, sir," I said carefully. "Her mouth was bloody."

"Can you control her without one?"

"I can," I said. I thought about the bridle I had made and wished I could just go get it—but that would tell him more than I wanted him to know.

"Wait here," the stablemaster said, and walked away from me. A few minutes later he was back with a bridle that had no bit—just a leathern headstall and reins. I slid it over Dannsair's muzzle. She stood still once she understood there was nothing going into her mouth.

That first day, the stablemaster just had me lead Dannsair in wide circles inside the town walls, back and forth across the open fields between the town and the stables. Then he had me get on, and he watched as I guided her at a walk, then a trot, and finally a canter. Then we took her back to the barn.

Leaving that evening, I was buoyed by hope. The baron wouldn't want to give Dannsair to me, but if his pride was staked on the race and I gave him the prize that the Baron of Galway was putting up...

I pressed my cheek against Dannsair's. If the Baron of Athenry agreed to it, all we had to do was win a race and I could go home, taking my filly with me.

CHAPTER THIRTEEN

❧ ❧ ❧

My mother comes each day now and takes me outside.
Every day is full of open fields and galloping.
I am so happy.

$\mathcal{T}$he stablemaster hired another boy to muck out stalls.

Fothud and Guaire both promised to shout for me in the race. I hoped they would. Their cheers would mean a great deal to me.

I told Old Brigit, of course, that I would be riding in the race and that if I won, I could have the filly I would be riding. I didn't tell her more than that, but she was so happy for me that she made a special supper of new greens and venison.

After we ate, she gave me a string of leather to tie

my hair back in a short tail that barely brushed the nape of my neck. She smiled, her eyes twinkling. "There, now you look a proper boy again—and you will be able to see where you are galloping."

I glanced at her, wondering if she knew I was a girl, but was too kind to pry into my secrets. She did not meet my eyes; she was already stirring the fire. We sat close together that night, happy with our comfortable silence as usual. I don't know what she was thinking about. I was dreaming of Dannsair and of being together—and free.

The next morning, rising early as I always did, I found Old Brigit up before me. She had boiled barley and buttered it. We ate together. "Learn well and I am sure you will win," she said. I carried those words with me to the barn that morning and every morning that followed.

"The baron has agreed," the stablemaster told me the moment he saw me.

I caught my breath, then danced a circle, and he laughed. Then I remembered to stand straight and lower my voice. "He is a man of his word and bond?"

The stablemaster nodded. "Of course." Then

he gestured. "Bridle the filly and come with me."

There was a small, enclosed paddock behind the castle that he used to teach young Norman boys to ride. It was also used for war practice. Older boys were shown how to fight with swords, how to hold their shields and move quickly beneath the weight of their chain mail.

They would practice elsewhere while we were there, though; the stablemaster ordered the paddock cleared while I learned to ride properly.

I loved going into the castle grounds every morning. Inside the circle of the high castle walls were many wonders. We passed gardens full of cabbage and celeriac and plants I had never seen before. There were chickens pecking for bugs, and among them was an odd, dark-speckled fowl I had never seen before. There was another kind that had a tail so magnificent that at first I could not believe it was real. Peacocks, the stablemaster called them. And I saw Norman girls riding. There was a small stable within the castle keep. They rode gracefully, laughing and playing games, their flower-colored gowns flouncing and falling with their horses' gaits.

"Canter her," the stablemaster usually said once we were inside the paddock.

I leaned forward, and Dannsair rose into a slow, rocking gait, her head high and her neck arched. I was careful to keep my weight in line with hers as I guided her in a wide circle. That was what he was teaching me. Not how to keep my balance, but to help Dannsair keep *hers*.

It was such a joy to ride Dannsair in the fresh air, to feel the sky above us, to smell the damp grass beneath her hooves. All I lacked was the wind in my hair to make it the dream I had had of riding all my life—and that was more for lack of hair than anything else. Thanks to Old Brigit's gift, I nearly always wore it tied back, now that it was long enough.

"Shift your weight forward again," the stable-master called to me. "Pull her up into a gallop with your knees and your belly, not your heels or your hands."

I heard laughter and glanced aside to see the three Norman boys. I quickly looked forward again.

"Begone!" the stablemaster shouted at them. They whirled and ran.

"Shift your weight forward," the stablemaster repeated. "Bring your knees up. You'll feel it when you are balanced where you should be. You will feel her stride lengthen."

I did as I was told, and I felt Dannsair lengthen her stride a little.

"That's right," the stablemaster called. "Keep her at that pace."

Dannsair was so glad to have more room, to be outside, that she galloped happily in a circle around the paddock for a long time—long enough to soak her shoulders with sweat.

When the stablemaster finally called to me to rein her in, I brought my weight back, then gently tightened the reins. She slowed, broke back into a trot, then stopped when I asked her to.

"Better than most," the stablemaster said as I turned Dannsair toward him. "Better than most are after a year of work." I thought he was talking about Dannsair, and I smiled. "You ride well," he added. "You have a gift, boy."

All my life I had wanted to ride. And I was *good* at it? I could not have been more happy. Then I spotted Niall walking with his father and remembered that his father worked for the baron. Niall had probably been inside the castle walls many times. He waved. I waved back, then looked away, squaring up my shoulders and lifting my chin.

"The baron won't like you riding bareback like some Irish rí's son, but he wants to win," the stablemaster said as I came close. "I will bring you proper clothes tomorrow." And so he did, if *Norman* meant *proper*. The next morning, he bade me dress in leggings and a tunic and meet him at the stables gate. As you may imagine, I waited for him to walk away, then I stood at the very back of Dannsair's stall and changed quickly.

The clothing felt very strange. I walked around, trying to get used to the stiff cloth of the tunic and the odd fit of the trousers. Then I led Dannsair out.

In the days that followed, I rode so much that my legs and back ached. For the first six days, we galloped hard in the castle paddock for hours at a time. I slowly got used to the Norman clothing, or at least I stopped noticing it so much.

Twice, I saw people watching from a window high in the castle. I once caught a glimpse of long white hair and knew it was the baron. I wanted to shout a thanks to him, but didn't dare.

On the seventh day, the stablemaster saddled a long-striding bay mare, and we rode side by side out the stables, past the town of Athenry, and out of the North Gate. Once we were well beyond the town walls, I spotted my holly tree.

"Ride ahead of me," the stablemaster said. "Keep the filly in hand. I will tell you where to go."

I let Dannsair have her head. I can barely tell you how I felt as we galloped along narrow paths that led uphill, then down, through dappled shade and flashing sunlight.

"Now follow the creek," the stablemaster called from behind me, and I guided Dannsair along a path beside the stream where I had bathed before I managed to enter Athenry town.

"Uphill!" he shouted, and I guided Dannsair to the side to follow a path that wound back and forth, always angling toward the top of the ridge. Coming back, we galloped right past my holly tree.

On the eighth day, six horses left the barn with us. I recognized two of the riders. One was the Norman boy who hated me for taking his place on Dannsair's back, and the other was Niall. I kept Dannsair out to one side, avoiding talking to any of them. I rode with my back straight and my chin up and my mind spinning with worry. The bigger the group of boys, the more I felt out of place.

Once we were outside the North Gate, with the town of Athenry and the castle behind us, the stablemaster explained the real racecourse to us. He led us all along it, riding at a walk, then again at an easy trot.

The course began—and finished—in the meadow just outside the North Gate. It arced in a long circle up over a ridge, then across a wide, flat field, then through the woods and back down.

The course was not too hard, and mostly flat. There were two steep upgrades that would tire the horses, and one sharp downhill that could hurt any horse pushed down it too fast. Dannsair was prancing, a little nervous around so many horses and people.

The stablemaster lined us up and had us start a mock race, each horse leaping from a standstill to top speed, galloping a short way, then doing it again. He rode back and forth, shouting instructions, mostly at me.

I learned to feel Dannsair's muscles bunch as she prepared to leap, and by the fifth or sixth time, we were breaking from the starting line ahead of all the other horses. I was already sitting forward as she leaped.

It was midmorning before I realized that the stablemaster was watching the other horses closely. Of course. He was selecting the baron's second entry in the race.

All the horses were fast, I was sure, but there was more to it than that. Niall was riding a tall sorrel that fought with him the whole time, refusing to turn, tossing his head. The Norman boy was on a dapple-gray mare. She seemed too nervous around the other horses, her ears always back, her eyes rimmed in white. The other riders were older, but not much. The stablemaster was obviously concerned with the weight each horse had to carry.

We rode the course at a hand gallop twice, not letting the horses go at a full gallop, then walked them back to the stables. I saw the stablemaster talking to a slight young man riding a chestnut courser. The chestnut had kept up with Dannsair easily—and I was sure that the stablemaster had made his choice.

As we rode back, no one said a word to me. Not even Niall. He was too busy fighting his mount, trying to keep him in hand.

I was grateful.

It was hard, pretending to be a boy, especially now, with so much at stake. These boys had no reason to do me a kindness—most of them probably resented me. They were there because they rode well, and they had all had learned their skills slowly and carefully. I had been a stall cleaner until eight days before. If anything about me seemed the least bit odd or suspicious, they would tell the stablemaster.

We rode mock race starts again the next day, with the stablemaster shouting two commands: "Be ready!" and "Ride!" to start each race. Dannsair learned the meaning of the words after four or five starts—it was simple enough for her. She had already learned other voice commands. That made it easy for me. I just sat still and readied myself to move with her when she burst into a gallop.

Then we rode the course at a canter twice. There would be watchers at every stretch. Cutting curves to shorten the distance meant being barred from winning.

It was hard to hold Dannsair back. She loved the galloping, and she wanted to be ahead of the other horses. The stablemaster pulled me aside.

"A race is won at the end, not the beginning," he said solemnly. He waited until I met his eyes to finish. "Never fall too far back to catch up, and never think being ahead before the finish line means you will win."

I nodded.

"And never cut the curves, even a little. No one who cheats will be allowed to win."

I nodded again and waited for him to say something more, but he didn't. We rode home slowly, and I saw what I had not noticed that morning in the dawn dusk. There were tents being raised at the far end of the meadow outside the town walls. The Irish entrants were arriving.

The next morning, I watched from a distance,

as the Irish riders were shown the course. There was a long-strided bay that worried me. It barely seemed to strike the ground with its hooves.

Looking past the horses, I noticed a boy standing near the holly tree I had hidden in. He had a mass of curly red hair.

Cormac?

I watched him walking, talking to another boy. It *was*.

I was astounded. Were people coming from that far away? I scanned the meadow and saw Conall, the Irishman who had captured me and Dannsair and kept us prisoners at his stables. He was off to one side, watching the horses.

I looked for Dannsair's sire, but he wasn't among the tethered horses. It made sense. Conall and Cormac's father wouldn't risk injuring a prize stallion in a race.

I felt foolish. I had assumed this race would be like the ones my father had held—a friendly contest between neighbors. Conall and Cormac would notice Dannsair, of course. But would they recognize me from a distance? I would look, with my short, tied-back hair and Norman clothes, like any Norman boy from Athenry. I kept telling myself that, and I began to believe it. They wouldn't know me unless I got too close.

The next few days were the hardest of all because there was very little for me to do except worry. The stablemaster allowed Dannsair and the chestnut courser light exercise in the morning, then insisted that both horses rest.

The town of Athenry bustled with people preparing for Beltaine—they had more food than my tuath ever had this time of year. The baron's hunters went out nearly every day, and the market was full of venison and boar meat.

"Give me something to do," I pleaded with Brigit one afternoon. "Before I worry myself ill."

She smiled and pointed to a pile of birch bark and, beside it, a linen sack of bogbean. "That all needs grinding. The man paying for the cloak wants dark colors to hide him from the deer he hunts so he can get closer." She arched her brows. "Perhaps he is not the best with a bow?"

We laughed together, then I set to work and was soon too tired to worry. Instead, I day-dreamed . . .

After the race, when Dannsair was mine, I would go home. My mother would be looking downhill from the rath and would see me riding toward her. Her face would light as I came close, then slid off Dannsair's back to embrace her. Bebinn, Gerroc, Magnus, and Tally, all my family, all my friends—it would be wonderful to see them. My father might still be home, not yet off fighting his endless battles. And there my thoughts stopped. Would my father take Dannsair from me?

He might.

I pounded at the bark, concentrating on the work, trying not to begin a second set of worries. Before anything else, I had to win the race.

CHAPTER FOURTEEN

🐎 🐎 🐎

I can scent strange horses, and I hear many strangers'
voices. I hope my mother will come soon so that we can be
out beneath the sky to gallop in the sunshine.

I led Dannsair out of the North Gate the
next morning, with the stablemaster
walking before me and the young man leading the
chestnut courser behind me. I scanned the
crowds in front of the line of tents, glancing at
the faces, then looked away, relieved.

I could not see their faces clearly. That meant
that none of them were close enough to get a
good look at me. The baron's men had kept the
crowds well away from the line where the race
would start and finish. Two posts had been set

up to mark it, the grass cleared between them.

There were sixteen horses. As we lined up, the crowd began to shout, cheering their favorites.

I laid one hand flat on Dannsair's neck.

She was trembling.

So was I. But I forced myself to calm down so that I could talk quietly to her.

"We are both very young, but you are the fastest horse here," I told her. I rubbed her silky neck and tugged gently at her mane, talking about how we would soon be able to go home. And all the while I was talking, I was remembering everything the stablemaster had taught me.

"*Be ready!*" A man wearing a bright blue coat shouted—and the whole meadow was suddenly as quiet as though no one stood there at all. I felt Dannsair's body tense; she knew what was coming.

"*Ride!*" the man shouted—and the crowd screamed and cheered as Dannsair sprang forward. She was a half stride out before any of the other horses moved at all. I sat tight, keeping my weight far forward over her neck and withers as Dannsair leaped into her second stride, then her third. Joy filled my heart as she settled into an even rhythm. We had started well and stayed clear of the other horses.

Dannsair's strides were effortless and long, but two other riders came even with us halfway across the meadow. One was the bay with the graceful, reaching stride. The boy who rode it was twice my size, but his horse looked strong enough to gallop all day. The other was a plain-faced dun mare with a choppy gait and a blunt muzzle.

I let my body move with Dannsair's, willing myself to balance so precisely that she would not have to waste any of her strength in carrying me.

The sound of the shouting crowd dimmed with distance, and the sound of hoofbeats seemed to get louder. Dannsair was running well, fast, but still in hand, her strides long but easy. None of the riders would be letting their horses go flat out yet.

As we neared the base of the long hill that led up the ridge, the sounds of the crowd were gone—there was only the sound of hoofbeats and the breathing of the horses.

I glanced back as we started up the slope. The horses had started in a bunch, but they were now in a line of twos and threes. Dannsair leaped up the hill, her ears forward. I let her go for a dozen strides before I gently brought her back to a steadier pace. She wanted to be in front the whole race. It was my task to keep her from wearing thin at the end.

I glanced back again. The incline had spaced the horses out even farther, the stronger ones surging forward.

Dannsair wanted to keep the lead, but I gently pulled her in, talking to her, settling my weight. Her ears flickered as she responded, checking her stride a little.

As we rode near the top of the ridge and the first turn in the course, the bay eased past us and the plain-faced horse came up close on the opposite side. I brought Dannsair back a little to keep her in the open, to try to keep her clear of the others. She shoved her muzzle forward, jerking the reins, and I understood: She didn't like giving up ground for any reason.

At the top of the ridge, after the wide turn, I let Dannsair go. She flattened out, lengthening her stride. I kept my weight over her withers, my body rounded, the reins loose.

The bay was still beside us, the rider sitting too straight, his weight too far back—or so I thought. But the horse was strong, a fully grown animal, and if his rider's weight was hard for him to carry, he showed no sign of it.

I pulled Dannsair back, and the bay's rider brought him in hand as well. The dun was close as we crossed the wide meadow, the others strung out behind. Some of the riders were using their whips now.

As we came around the second turn, the plain-faced dun took the lead, galloping hard, neck outstretched and breathing loudly. Next was the big bay, still going easily, his long stride eating up the earth.

Dannsair and I came next. I noticed a course watcher for the first time as we galloped past, and I was careful not to cut any of the curves short as we all followed the big arc of the third turn and started down the face of the ridge.

There were now thirteen horses strung out in a long line behind three horses that were running nearly shoulder to shoulder: Dannsair, the dun, and the long-strided bay.

Dannsair was in the middle. It scared me to have the others so close, but I was afraid to pull her back as she plunged down the steepening slope. The bay was running easily, and the dun kept up with him—though I saw her rider using a whip.

I let Dannsair out a little, and the other two let me take the lead, probably hoping that we would fall back at the end.

I knew what Dannsair could do, and I wasn't worried about her stamina. What I didn't know was how the other two ran. If the dun needed whipping to keep up now, was she tired, or just a little stubborn? Was the bay as tireless as he looked?

The steep incline was coming up. I let Dannsair out a little more, and risked a quick glance back. Besides the bay and the dun, there was a roan not too far behind us, and two horses just behind the roan. The rest were out of the race for good and all.

I fixed my eyes on the path ahead and loosened the reins so that Dannsair could keep her balance on the slope. Every stride jolted us both now, her forelegs hitting hard.

The steepest place came up quicker than I

expected, but Dannsair seemed to know where it was. She checked her stride without my asking her to, then plunged downward. I shifted my weight back, helping her as best I could.

I heard a sudden shout from behind us and glanced back to see the dun sliding sideways, then crashing to its knees. Scared, hoping the horse and rider were all right, I guided Dannsair to the side of the path as far as I dared, where the earth was softer and the footing was better. It slowed her down, and I didn't care.

At the bottom, I sat forward, my eyes straight ahead. Dannsair responded to me leaning forward with a burst of speed.

I heard the big bay's breathing behind us, and I saw him out of the corner of my eye. His rider was using the ends of the reins now, too, lashing his flanks. The bay leaped forward.

I leaned low over Dannsair's neck, and she kept her lead, barely, as we rounded the last long turn and thundered back across the meadow toward Athenry, riding hard.

Shouts and cheers rose from the crowd, and it startled Dannsair. I could feel her shortening her stride, and the bay came up beside us, his long legs gaining a little ground every stride.

"Ride!" I said to Dannsair, and she sprang off her hindquarters as though the race were just beginning, hurtling us forward, making up the lost ground, then moving ahead of the bay.

The bay's rider was working the reins, lashing his horse's flanks, but Dannsair was hunched, her neck flat and low, digging into the dirt with every stride. We galloped across the finish line with the bay two horse lengths behind us, and the others strung out even farther.

I loosed the reins and sat back, letting Dannsair slow gradually, turning her gently to one side in a long circle as she brought herself back into a canter, then a trot.

I saw the stablemaster gesturing at me to ride closer, and I pretended not to see him. The crowd was still cheering, and I raised one arm to let them know I heard them. They roared, all of them, the Irish and Normans alike. Dannsair was owned by the baron, and her rider looked Norman, but she was Irish-sired, and everyone had probably heard the story by now.

My heart was pounding. I could barely believe it. We had won! I cantered around the edge of the cheering crowd hoping to see Old Brigit, but I couldn't spot her. Afraid that Conall or Cormac might recognize me if I got any closer, I turned Dannsair toward the North Gate. The guards cheered, and I smiled up at them as my filly and I entered the town of Athenry.

"We won!" I whispered to Dannsair. "We can go home." Sudden tears flooded my eyes, and I could not stop them.

I didn't even try. No one would see.

The whole town was back in that meadow, cheering for my filly, for Beltaine's promise of summer, for the end of Gam and its cold rains, for life and love and everything good.

CHAPTER FIFTEEN

᪥ ᪥ ᪥

*There is nothing better than a long gallop in the cool hours
of morning. I am faster than the others that ran today,
and that pleases me. My mother is pleased, too. I can tell.
I hope we can gallop again soon.*

I was just entering the maze of paths that ran between the craftsmen's byres and the Irish houses. It was strange to see the town of Athenry so still, so empty. I had used my sleeve to dry my face, and Dannsair's sweat was cooling on her shoulders when I saw someone running toward me.

I hesitated, then recognized Niall. I shook my head, hoping he would understand and leave me alone. I didn't want him asking me how the race had felt or whether it was exciting or anything else. He slowed enough not to startle Dannsair, but came closer.

"I heard my father talking about the race with the baron," he said to me between breaths.

I reined in. "Niall," I said impatiently, "I have to rub her down and—"

"They intend to cheat you," he cut me off.

I stared at him. "What do you mean?"

"They aren't going to give you the filly or the prize. They aren't even going to give you back your job as a stall cleaner. They don't want you around the filly anymore. They don't want anyone to know they used an Irish rider."

"Trian!"

The stablemaster's shout was faint with distance, but it startled us both. I turned to see him striding up the road just inside the North Gate. I knew in that instant that Niall was right, and I was furious with myself. I had wanted the lies to be true so much that I had believed them.

"I thank you, and will repay you someday," I said to Niall. "He can't see you because Dannsair is in the way. Run now and he won't."

Niall nodded and wished me luck, then he

took off, sprinting back between two houses, out of sight.

"Trian!" the stablemaster shouted again. "Wait!"

I turned and faced him, Dannsair still breathing deep, her head down with weariness.

The stablemaster finally reached us, and he looked carefully at Dannsair. "Is she all right?"

"She went perfectly," I told him, and smiled widely. Everything made sense now, including the Norman clothes. It embarrassed him to have an Irish rider—and he wouldn't want anyone to believe me if I told.

"You did well," he said. "Go rest. I will take care of her."

"Thank you," I said, "but I want to rub her down and get her supper once she is cooled off. She's mine now, and I want to be careful of her."

He hesitated, and I pleaded with the saints and the faeries to help me convince him that I still believed the lie. They must have listened because he smiled at me, a false, brittle smile.

"All right," he said. "I'll see you in the morning." He gestured toward the castle. "The baron has opened his doors—my family will be at his feast this year. He is most pleased to have won the race." His happiness at that seemed genuine at least.

I dismounted and pretended to lead Dannsair toward the barns until he had walked out of sight. Then I started shaking. It was fury, but it was desperation, too. What would I do? What *could* I do?

Two or three hundred people had just watched me, dressed in Norman clothes, ride a moon-colored filly in a race. I would not be able to ride back out among them without the baron's men stopping me.

I wanted to scream at the sky. It was so unfair. It was wrong. Once more, someone meant to take my filly away from me.

"If you were a dun or a bay, we might manage to slip out the gates after the baron's feast begins," I told her. "But how can I possibly hide a moon-colored—" Then I stopped talking because I knew what to do.

Running, I led Dannsair straight into the empty maze of paths—every living soul had gone to the meadow outside the walls to watch the race. We turned left, then right, then left again, and I finally led her through the doorway of Old Brigit's house. The horse was weary and stood quietly among the looms. I moved them aside and then set to work.

I had the bogbean and birch bark pounded into dust by the time Old Brigit came home. Her eyes widened when she saw Dannsair, and her smile of congratulations dimmed. "What, Trian? What is wrong?"

I told her the whole story, and her face darkened.

"He will keep the prize, I am sure," I said angrily. "And I will keep his bargain whether he is honest enough to honor it or not."

She was shaking her head. "The Normans are not all like the baron," she said. "But he rules them, and his men will never let you leave."

"I will need your help," I said.

She nodded. "I will give it."

I explained my idea and she nodded again, her eyes shining. "It should work."

"I wish I could wear my leine." I gestured at

the Norman clothes the stablemaster had given me. "But if I wear the leine you made, people will know I am Irish, and they might wonder where an Irish boy got such a fine horse."

"Ah," she said. "There is a way around that."

❧ ❧ ❧

Old Brigit helped me mix wheat meal into the dye pot. Then we pressed the sticky mixture into Dannsair's coat, covering every bit of her body except her forehead. She didn't like it, and she was restless while the dye soaked in, but she was very tired, and Old Brigit fed her oats and talked to her while I gathered my things.

Once I was ready, I kissed Brigit's wrinkled cheek and hugged her tightly. She held me at arm's length and laughed. "It is a grand joke." Her eyes were twinkling. "A girl pretending to be a boy pretending to be a girl!"

I stared at her, surprised and ashamed that I had lied to such a good friend.

"Tell me your given name, dear girl," she whispered.

I hesitated only an instant. "Larach. And I

thank you with all my heart." We embraced again and for once I could cry freely.

❦ ❦ ❦

And so, a little before dusk, a girl with her too-short hair braided and tied back into a lacy hood, wearing a beautiful blue-green dress, rode a dull brown filly out of the North Gate. The horse was under a Norman saddle, and it wore an odd tablet-woven bridle of good craftsmanship. The rider and her horse were surrounded by crowds of people celebrating.

No one noticed.

No one cared.

Dannsair walked slowly, her coat smelling of bogberry, but dry and clean. I sat up straight on the saddle Old Brigit had given me, wearing her blue wedding dress, my bag of belongings tied to the back of the saddle. I had saved thirty silver pennies. I had left them all in Old Brigit's larder, next to a sack of oats. It was not enough, but it was all I had, and I hoped she would understand how grateful I was.

Dannsair and I ambled along in the twilight,

crossing the meadow slowly, keeping well away from the Irish tents.

I saw Cormac on my way—he was standing beside a fire, looking up at the stars. He glanced my way abruptly, as though he had heard someone call his name.

I faced forward. Dannsair was tired, and her head was lower than usual, and I had to nudge her to walk faster. I kept going, and I did not look back.

I rode west. I had no idea where I was going, but it didn't scare me. After all, I was riding the best filly in Ireland.